THE GOON AND THE GLASS SWAN

THE GOON AND THE GLASS SWAN

AND FIVE OTHER TALES

SCOTT WILLIAM CARTER

CONTENTS

Visit our website at *www.flyingravenpress.com* for more information about this book and other titles for sale.

THE GOON AND THE GLASS SWAN

THEY CALLED HIM GOON. Not *the* Goon. Just Goon, as if it was his name, which it sort of was. Or maybe as if he wasn't even worthy of the article in front of the insult, which also might have been true. They thought he was stupid, but he wasn't, at least not nearly as stupid as they made him out to be. He was a goon, though. There was no doubt about that. He was ugly, he was a thug, and he was no good. What else did it take to make a goon?

Only three people in his whole life had ever called him by his real name, at least anybody who mattered: his mother, God rest her soul; Maggie, the pretty brunette from the laundromat; and Nick, who'd sort of raised him since Goon's mother died snorting coke with a Wall Streeter on the Upper East Side when Goon was four. He didn't remember much about her, except that she'd taught him to read before he could even tie his shoes.

Oh, and that she was pretty. Like Maggie.

"Listen to me, Glen," Nick said, screwing the suppressor onto his Ruger Mark IV. The squeak of metal on metal was barely audible over the hum of the elevator. The suppressor was the same dull black as Nick's plastic gloves. "This one might get messy, okay? He likes his whores and there might be a couple around, but nothing we can do about it, they got to be iced too. The reason we're coming on Sunday is I figure it be the one day Johnny Two Pair might keep his pecker in his pants, being the good Catholic boy he is, but there are no guarantees, you know? You understand me, Glen? I gotta hear that you understand me."

"You got it, boss," Goon said. He liked it when Nick used his real name, but it was hard thinking of himself as Glen when he was on a job. He wasn't packing, but that was fine, his weapons of choice were permanently attached to his body. Unlike Nick, he wore leather gloves; plastic would just rip if he had to punch somebody. "It won't be a problem, I *swear*," he added.

Nick nodded, staring down the long barrel at his reflection in the elevator's mirrored walls. His unnaturally blond hair, styled with enough hairspray to make it stick up like a candle flame, was getting thin around Nick's temples, but Goon was careful never to say this. Nick was sensitive about his looks, way more than Goon, who'd long since accepted his ugliness but still tried not to look at himself as they rode up in the elevator. It was hard not to, when the mirrors were on all sides and Goon was so big he filled most of them.

It was a nice elevator, with cherry wainscotting below the mirrors, a brass rail almost as reflective as the glass, and green-patterned carpet that must have been new, because it still smelled like glue.

"I can't have another situation like what happened on Staten Island," Nick said finally. "I just can't, you got me?"

"I know. It won't, I *promise*."

Goon was really laying the Lennie voice on thick, something he was careful not to overdo, but he sometimes wondered if it would matter even if he played the part with all the gusto of an off-off-off Broadway performer on stage for the first time. Since everybody in Goon's life—well, everybody but one —*wanted* to believe he was stupid, no amount of overacting would probably change their minds. Lennie was the dumb brute from John Steinbeck's *Of Mice and Men*, a book Goon read when he was nine. That was when he realized that not only was he Lennie, he was also Lennie's smart friend George. He was both at the same time.

But he figured out pretty quickly that it was better, and safer, if the world only got to see the Lennie side of him. It gave Goon options, different ways of dealing with people. That even included Nick.

"Yeah, well," Nick was saying now, "you promised

me the same thing last time. We almost died when that bitch pulled a snubbie out of her couch. And you just standing there like a dumb ox. If I told Milo about what happened on Staten Island, he'd yank you back to bouncing at The Corner Pocket in a hot minute, you hear me? Is that what you want, standing on your bad arches all night, eyes burning from all the cigarette smoke, and nothing to do but keep drunks from putting their hands on the strippers?"

"No, sir," Goon said.

"Damn straight. It happens again, I ain't gonna lie for you. It hurts me to say so, 'cause you're like a brother to me, but I gotta be able to count on you, right?"

"Right."

"Good. Make sure you remember it when it matters. Hey, you want to do Coney Island on Saturday? Ride the Hurricane, eat some taffy, feed the pigeons?"

Goon smiled his biggest, goofiest smile. The truth was, he was getting tired of pretending the stuff that entertained him when he was eight was the same stuff that entertained him twenty years later—these days, he'd rather take in a Broadway show than ride a rickety old roller coaster—but he knew these outings did something for Nick, who would never be able to admit that he actually enjoyed Coney Island himself. "Sure, boss!" Goon said, with as much glee as he could muster. "That'd be fun."

"Cool. Okay, same plan as always: I focus on the

mark. You cover me on the way in, then you sweep the place while I keep Johnny Two Pair in line. You find any whores, you bring 'em out front, right?"

"Right."

"No funny business, Glen. He's thinking we're just here to get the package for Milo, maybe a little social visit, so it should be easy peasy, but you never know. Okay, show time."

The elevator shuddered, then chimed. Penthouse suite. They faced the elevator doors, Nick with his Ruger at his side and slightly behind his leather trench coat. The last time Goon had come here, he remembered a foyer with fake geraniums on marble pillars flanking Johnny Two Pair's door, gaudy stuff. That was still the case when the elevator doors rumbled open, but instead of having to knock and wait, Johnny Two Pair was already standing in the open doorway.

In white silk pajamas, no less. Against the white silk, his skin looked like dark bronze. He was a big guy but not much taller than Nick; his pajamas stretched taut against bulging pecs and thighs. His black fifties pompadour was perfectly styled. When he smiled, which he did now, his fake teeth were so long that they always made Goon think of piano keys, especially because they were darker at the top because he'd gotten the crowns from some back-alley dentist in South America.

Johnny held up a martini glass filled with blue,

crushed ice. "Hey, Nick, my man, I got your favorite martini right ..."

The words trailed off when Nick stuck the suppressor in the middle of Johnny's forehead. Nick was fast with a gun, faster than anyone Goon had ever seen. Then, before Johnny could even gurgle another word, Nick walked the two of them into Johnny's place.

Scanning the room, seeing no one else, Goon closed the door behind them. Adele was singing "Hello" in a voice so rich and soulful it was like she was in the room. It was a nice place, with a sweeping view of the Hudson from the corner windows, though the mix of white leather couches and midcentury modern furniture was a little odd. Then again, all wise guys were odd. Nick's own music of choice was the Backstreet Boys. Who the hell still listened to the Backstreet Boys? Who had *ever* listened to the Backstreet Boys?

"What the hell, Nick!" Johnny finally managed.

"Shut up," Nick said. No shouting. Nick almost never shouted, and he especially didn't shout on a job. "Get on your knees."

"What?"

Nick slapped him with his left hand. So far, Johnny had miraculously managed to hold onto the martini, but now it went flying and shattered on the slate stone floor. The glass didn't go far, but the blue liquid sure did—the white leather, the walnut end table, and all over Johnny Two Pair's bare feet. Fortunately, it didn't get on the brown paper sack perched on the coffee table, which undoubtedly contained the package they'd ostensibly come to collect. Full of cash for Milo, no doubt.

Most people thought Johnny Two Pair's name had to do with poker, which would have been a good guess given Johnny burned through a lot of dough playing Texas Hold 'Em in Atlantic City, but the truth was much stranger. They called him Johnny Two Pair because apparently his left and right feet were so different that he had to order different shoes, so two pairs instead of one. This was the first time Goon had ever seen the guy in his bare feet, so he took a good look at them.

They seemed the same to him. Probably just another bullshit story. Even more than money and whores, wise guys loved their bullshit stories.

"Christ!" Johnny cried, rubbing his already reddening cheek. "Christ, Nick!"

Nick motioned to the floor with the Ruger. "On your knees or I'll shoot you in the gut instead of putting one between your eyes. You want to bleed out or die quick? Choice is yours."

That was the moment when it must have finally occurred to Johnny that this was no package pick-up or social visit—that this was, in fact, the last visit of any sort he was ever going to have. He started to blubber and cry, which was pathetic, but it was also riveting. It always amazed Goon how guys like Johnny Two Pair could act so tough and then turn into babies as soon as they were at the other end of the gun.

It wasn't until Nick glared at Goon that he finally snapped out of it and made a hasty exit toward the hall, which led to the kitchen, the bedroom, and the rest of the house. It smelled of pepper steak and cooked asparagus. Resting on the gray granite kitchen counter was a single, dirty plate, as well as a glass empty except for melting ice cubes. One plate, one glass. Good signs.

As Goon swept through the kitchen, then the bathroom, checking closets and cabinets, he could make out Johnny Two Shoe begging for his life.

"You don't have to do this, Nick!"

"Afraid I do, Johnny."

"But I got Milo's package! I got it right—"

"Don't matter. Milo found out about your little side hustle in Key West. Or did you think you could keep that secret? Sneaking in your own girls?" He clucked disapprovingly.

"Please, Nick. I—I got extra. I been s-s-squirreling some away. I can pay you as much as—"

"Shut up! I ain't dirty, unlike some guys, so don't make this worse. Just take it like a man. You can do that, can't you, Johnny? You can act like a man at least here at the end?"

Then Goon was out of earshot, but it didn't really matter, because Johnny was sobbing so much that it was impossible to make out what he was saying anyway. There were two bedrooms, both with closed doors, so Goon was careful when he opened them. The one on the left was the master, with its own magnificent view of both the river and much of the West Village, all of it glittering in the early Fall night. The ensuite and its walk-through closet alone were bigger than Goon's flat in Brooklyn. White marble counters. Terra cotta tiles. The works. There were more men's shoes than Goon had ever seen in one place, but no whores.

Goon checked the shoes and was surprised to find the story wasn't bullshit after all. The left were size ten, the right size eleven. That raised an interesting question. What did Johnny Two Pair do with all the unused halves? Toss them in the dumpster? Donate them to amputees? What?

While the master showed no sign of recent activity, the spare bedroom told a different story—and right from the moment he opened the door. A candle in beveled green glass burned on the nightstand, the cedar scent so strong it had obviously been going awhile. The bed was made, but there were sex toys laid out on the downy white bedspread in a neat and tidy fashion, like they were presented for a potential buyer.

There was nobody there, but the closet was closed. Goon checked under the bed, saw nothing, then stood to the left of the closet door and swung it open, careful to stay out of the path of a potential bullet.

Nobody shot at him. He did, however, get an

answer to the great shoe mystery. Below puffy parkas, sheepskin-lined bomber jackets, and heavy trench coats fit for New England winters, was a huge pile of shoes. A mountain, really. Unlike in the master, where the shoes were laid out as if on display at Macy's, these looked like they'd been tossed in haphazardly. It smelled of rubber, leather, and mothballs. Again, no whores, much to Goon's relief.

Satisfied, he started to close the door when something green caught his eye.

It was inside the pile of shoes. It wasn't so much the green that grabbed his attention as that the green momentarily disappeared before appearing again. Goon swallowed. He squatted on his haunches and carefully removed an Italian loafer, one that still contained its cardboard insert.

A pair of green eyes peered out at him.

If the eyes had been brown, he might not have noticed them originally, because of all that leather, but the green really stood out. It wasn't just that they were green. They were the greenest green he'd ever seen—not green like emeralds, but green like pine needles, grassy pastures, and the leaves of the maples outside his Brooklyn window in the heart of summer. It was the color of Goon's dreams, for he'd often fantasized about moving somewhere lush and green. Far from New York. Far from Nick, Milo, and all the terrible things he'd done.

Goon removed a few shoes. A pale, freckled cheek came into view. He cleared out a few more and revealed a strand of curly red hair. Then a bunch of shoes came tumbling down, and he jerked back in surprise, partly at the impromptu avalanche, and partly at what lay underneath all of Johnny Two Pair's discards.

It was a girl.

Not a girl as in a woman, the way a lot of guys referred to any broad they could imagine taking to bed, but an actual girl—a little thing dressed in a pink spaghetti strap shirt and denim shorts with a fraying hem. She cowered into herself, tucking spindly freckled arms around spindly freckled legs, a mop of orphan Annie hair spilling over her face.

She couldn't have been more than seven. Jesus. Goon felt bile rising into his throat.

"Goon?" Nick called from out front. "What the hell's taking so long?"

The girl looked up, blinking at him with her enormous green eyes. Goon had a decision to make, and he had to make it fast. If he brought the girl out now, Nick *might* let her live, because she hadn't actually witnessed a crime yet, and Nick had let some innocent bystanders go in the past. That was only when he didn't have to kill anybody, though. Since Nick was going to ice Johnny Two Pair no matter what, there *would* be a murder tonight, and that meant the girl, if she lived, could say that they'd been here.

There was an even worse fate for her, where she would be shipped overseas and bandied about by men even more vile than Johnny Two Pair, but Goon didn't want to think about that. It was bad enough, seeing her hiding in here with sex toys laid out on the bed.

Then the girl did something unexpected. She raised her right hand, and he saw that she was holding something—a tiny glass figurine. It was a swan. She held it out to him the way she might offer him a piece of candy. Her green eyes were still wide but they were not fearful. There was something hopeful about them, the green of the sea on a warm beach, the green of a wool blanket on a cold night, and Goon, staring back at those eyes, felt something change inside of him. It was like a gear, long out of whack, finally clicking into place.

He took the swan.

SIX MONTHS EARLIER, Goon was reading in the laundromat when Maggie walked into his life for the first time.

He was alone. It was going on ten o'clock on a Tuesday, late enough that he really didn't expect anyone else to show up, especially because it was raining so hard he probably could have just tossed his clothes on the sidewalk with a cup of detergent and saved himself some money. It had been raining like this for days. It was raining so much that it was hard to imagine it *not* raining, but it was only a week ago that Goon couldn't imagine the dirty snow that had plagued his Brooklyn neighborhood since early February ever going away either. The weather was funny that way.

He was chewing orange gum to help cover the smell of bleach. The sidewalk, lit from the laundromat windows, gleamed like chrome under the steady patter, but beyond the reach of the light the road was a black chasm. The lighted windows in the brownstones across the street were yellow smudges. His machines were the only ones running, a load in the washer, a load in the dryer, and he always found the sound soothing, but today he could barely hear them over the downpour.

Maybe it was the rain. Maybe it was the washer. Maybe it was just that he was so engrossed in his book that the outside world disappeared, but he didn't notice that a woman had stepped into the laundromat.

"Oh, hello," she said.

Her greeting startled him enough that he actually dropped his book—or rather the book inside the fake dust jacket that he'd used to hide the real book underneath. The hardcover slid out of the jacket and thumped against the yellow tiles. He snatched it up, embarrassed, but not so much because he'd dropped the book but because she'd surprised him. Goon was not used to being surprised. In his line of work, being surprised could get you killed.

When he finally looked at her, though, he was startled a second time, but not in a bad way. The brunette in the doorway, holding a blue laundry basket piled high with clothes, might have been the most beautiful woman he'd ever seen. Even with smeared mascara and wet hair matted to her scalp, she was mesmerizing.

She was a tiny, bird-like creature, with a long neck and high cheekbones. Her gray hoodie was soaked, but even this enhanced her attractiveness; the wet cotton clung to a fit and slender figure. Her eyes were very dark. Whatever embarrassment Goon felt was washed away as surely as the grime in the gutters, replaced by an attraction so intense that he immediately tried to quash it.

There was no way a woman like *that* would be with a guy like him. Not in a million years.

"Howdy," he said, grinning just a little, careful not to make too much eye contact. From a stranger, most people found too big a smile and too much eye contact unnerving enough. And from Goon? It was downright terrifying. One of the best ways to put people at ease, he'd found, was to make a self-deprecating remark. "Man, I'm such a klutz. Always dropping stuff. You got your pick of the litter tonight." He nodded toward the empty machines.

"Looks like it," she said. "About having my pick. Not about you being a klutz. I'm not one to talk, though."

She laughed, and it was a warm, rich laugh, not a nervous chuckle, nothing forced, and that was probably the moment Goon fell in love with her. It was also the moment when he felt more desperately lonely than he'd felt in his entire life, even when he'd finally realized that his mother was never coming back, because the intensity of his longing in the laundromat only made his absolute certainty that someone like *her* would never be with someone like *him* that much more painful.

Figuring she'd want to be left alone, he went back to reading his book and chewing his gum. Since the place was empty, and Goon was in the far back corner, he figured the woman would choose a machine on the other side. He was surprised when she took the one next to his.

Still, he did his best not to look at her as she loaded the washer—and it was a struggle *not* to look at her, the way her hips filled out her jeans—until she sat down two seats away from him. This might not have raised any questions if the place was filled, but it was hard to ignore when it was deserted.

"Man, it sure smells in here," she said.

"It does," he said.

"You got any spare gum?"

"What?"

"Gum. You're chewing gum."

"Oh, right."

"Only if you have extra."

"Sure, sure, no problem."

He set his book on his lap and fished out the Trident pack, which he held out to her. When she leaned over to take it, he caught a scent of vanilla—

perfume, lotion, it was hard to say—strong enough that he smelled it even over the bleach and his own orange gum.

After she took a stick, he went back to reading, still figuring she was just being polite. It was kind of nuts, a woman coming here alone so late and sitting next to a guy like him, but maybe being friendly was her way of calming her nerves, so the best thing he could do was be nonthreatening. But that lotion. Man. It was going to drive him nuts.

He glanced over the top of his book at the time left on his washer. Ten minutes. He had another hour or so of drying after that, but he wondered if he should just take his clothes home and hang dry them. Of course, that would be leaving her alone. Would that really be better?

"What are you reading?" she asked. "If you don't mind my asking. I'm a reader too. Always looking for a good author."

Boy, was this woman bold. He closed the book again, staring down at the stupid picture of the stupid actor on the cover, trying to remind himself what crazy ass stuff the guy had done over the years that might end up in a book like this, and drew a complete blank. He couldn't remember a single thing. He couldn't even remember any movies the guy had been in. All he could think about was the smell of vanilla.

What was up with this woman? Was she a hooker trying to solicit him? She didn't act like a hooker. She didn't have the vibe. Plus no hooker with two brain cells in her head would ever come into a place like this late at night by herself with a guy like him sitting alone at the back. She'd take one look at him and spin on her heels.

Then, when he looked over at her, he saw something he hadn't noticed before: a purple blotch on her left cheek, just below her eye. The darkness of the bruise meant it was recent, but the lack of puffiness meant it probably hadn't happened today. Yesterday, maybe. She obviously tried to hide the bruise with makeup, but the rain had washed much of her efforts away.

She must have misread the long pause as he studied her face, because she raised her hands apologetically. "Sorry, I don't mean to bother you," she said.

"No, no, it's fine."

"I know I talk too much sometimes. Everybody tells me that. Cute guy like you, you probably come in here late so girls don't bother you, and here I am bothering you. I should just let you read in peace."

He was struck speechless. Cute guy. Jesus. She actually called him a cute guy. She couldn't mean that.

"Oh, you know, it's just ... a book about some dumb actor." He was doing his best to use his Lennie voice, but it was a real struggle. Right from the start, he wanted to act like his Glen self with this girl, he didn't know why. "It's kind of stupid, I know, but sometimes I'm just sort of, I don't know in the mood for something trashy and—"

Before he could finish, she snatched it away from him. She was fast with her hands, almost as fast as Nick was with a gun. She studied the book, first smiling, then frowning, then smiling a bit wider before she looked at him again with her eyebrows raised.

"Ray Bradbury?" she said.

"Yeah."

"You're reading Ray Bradbury."

"I am."

She examined the book again. "*The Illustrated Man.* I remember this story collection. Ha. You're reading 'The Long Rain.' That's funny, considering the weather. Good story too."

He was surprised. "You've read it?"

"Sure I have. I love Bradbury. I like *Fahrenheit 451* best, but I love his short stories too. *The Martian Chronicles* is amazing." She shook her head and handed the book back to him. "I'm Maggie, by the way."

"Oh. Nice to meet you."

"You got a name?"

"Oh, it's ... Glen."

She laughed. "Are you sure?"

"Yeah. Sorry. I'm just, um, nervous, I guess."

"Nervous? Why would you be nervous?"

"Um, I just mean ... I don't ..."

She laughed again. "I'm just messing with you.

Okay, so I gotta ask. Why are you pretending to read a book about a scuzzy actor who's more famous for punching paparazzi than for any movies he made? I mean, most people, it's the other way around. Is it some weird way to pick up girls?"

"No, no, it's nothing like—"

"I'm just messing with you again."

"Oh. Right."

"But I really do want to know. Why pretend?"

She *did* want to know too. He could tell, by the way she was leaning halfway into the seat between them and her eyes were wide and focused intently on his. So wide and so dark. Unfathomably wide and dark. He could lose himself for eternity if he looked into those eyes for too long.

He wanted to tell her the truth, but he was afraid —partly afraid because he knew it could be dangerous for her, but mostly because he knew that if he opened up about *this,* then he might open up about other things, things he'd never told anyone, and where would that get him?

He could, however, give her a way out. "Tell you what," he said, dropping even a pretense of his Lennie voice, "I'll answer that question if you answer one of mine. Why do you have that bruise on your cheek?"

Glen—and for once, he thought of himself as Glen, not Goon—expected her to wilt away from him. He expected her to lean back into her plastic chair, stare at her clothes whirring in the washing machine, and let it go. Maybe she'd shed a tear. Maybe she'd leave in a huff.

She did none of those things. She did swallow, and her neck was so long and thin that he could actually track the movement, but she didn't look away.

"Sometimes it's just easier," she said, "if I'm somewhere else when he comes home."

THE SWAN WAS A TINY, precious thing. The glass was smooth and, even through his glove, Goon could feel the warmth from the girl's touch. The contrast between the leather and the glass was stark. Light on darkness. The tail feathers were finely detailed. The swan was surprisingly heavy for such a miniscule thing, small enough to fit entirely into his palm. Still, there was no doubt it was fragile. The neck was long and slender, the head bent back in on itself but not quite touching the body. If he dropped it, that neck would surely break.

There was something about the glass, the way the light, even in the dimly-lit closet, flowed inside it like a living thing, that mesmerized him, made him lose himself in the shimmers and sparkles.

"Goon?"

Nick's voice, louder this time, snapped him out of his trance. The girl's gaze flitted toward the door, then back at him, expectant, afraid. Goon made his decision. He closed his glove around the glass swan, then raised the same hand and pressed his extended finger to his lips. The girl nodded. He closed the door, easing the knob into place so it would make no sound, then made his way back to the living room.

He was careful not to look like he was in any kind of hurry. Nick, still pointing the Ruger at a kneeling Johnny, scowled at him.

"What the hell you doing back there?" he said. "Whacking off or something?"

"Just looking around, boss."

"No whores?"

"No. There's some candles burning in one of the bedrooms, and some sex toys out, but if somebody was here, they're gone now."

Nick looked at Johnny Two Pair, whose face was so red and puffy that he hardly looked like the same guy anymore. Judging by the wet spot on his robe and the puddle on the bamboo floor, he'd also pissed himself.

"That true, Johnny?" Nick said. "There ain't nobody hiding in here, is there? You want them to live, you better tell me now."

Goon tensed. It was a lie, and surely Johnny Two Pair knew it was a lie, but there was no telling what stupid thing he might say or do to save himself. When he swallowed and looked back and forth between Nick and Goon, Goon gave his head a little shake, but Johnny didn't seem to notice, and Goon was afraid to do more.

Face puffed up and pink, snot running down his

nose, Johnny Two Pair couldn't have looked more pathetic, and the thought of this fake tough guy with his fake tan putting his greasy hands on the little girl in the closet was so revolting that Goon wanted to rip his arms off, but he held himself in check.

"I never touched her," Johnny said. "Nobody's touched her. She's still clean."

Nick grimaced and looked at Goon. "What the hell is he talking about?"

"Hell if I know," Goon said.

"I thought you said nobody was back there?"

"There ain't. Not unless they can stuff themselves in one of the guy's shoes. Man, he's got a lot of shoes."

He tried to laugh, but his throat was too tight and his pulse was too fast, so it came out as a sort of whine. Nick gave him a funny look and turned his attention back to Johnny. Goon's heart was really going now, like fireworks, like cannons, like a wrecking ball laying waste inside his chest, and it was so loud he couldn't hear Adele, let alone what Nick was now saying to Johnny. He only knew that whatever Johnny said next, the game would be up for the girl in the closet, that was an absolute certainty, and so Goon did the only thing he could to shut Johnny Two Pair up. The only thing he was really good at.

He punched Johnny Two Pair in the face.

He didn't hold anything back either. It was just a right cross, nothing special, but he'd learned long ago that if he didn't hold back, he could kill somebody with one punch, and so he was usually careful with his power. He showed no such restraint here, however. Johnny Two Pair's head slapped backward and cracked against the stone floor with a sickening crunch.

Johnny didn't move. He didn't get up. He might as well have been a sack of dirty laundry for how still he was, except there was now blood pouring from his nose. What was left of his nose. For a long time, Nick just stared down the barrel of his Ruger, then he turned, slowly, and gave Goon the same look he used to give him when Goon was ten and Nick caught him in the middle of the night eating a whole package of Oreos.

"What the hell did you do that for?" Nick said. Annoyed, but not raising his voice. "Shit, man."

"Felt like it," Goon said.

"He was supposed to be awake when I iced him. Milo said so. You might have even killed him."

"Sorry."

But he wasn't. Goon hated to kill people—really, really hated to kill people—but he didn't feel any remorse about killing Johnny Two Pair. Nick sighed and fired two quick shots into the middle of Johnny Two Pair's forehead. He did it the way he might have changed the channel with a remote.

Then he snatched the brown paper sack off the coffee table, briefly peered inside, then rolled the whole thing up and stuffed it inside his jacket.

"Let's bolt," he said. "Shit, man, you never make it easy for me."

They headed for the door. For the first time since Goon found the girl, his heart began to slow. He figured the cops would eventually find her. What if the cops didn't, though? Goon would make sure. Later, after Nick dropped him off at his flat, Goon would walk down to the payphone next to the bagel shop. He'd tell the cops about the girl. Anonymously, of course. He'd tell them they should probably put her in witness protection, just to be safe. It would turn out all right.

Nick, reaching for the door handle, grinned at Goon.

"You gonna hit me, pal?"

"Huh?"

Nick glanced down at Goon's right hand. He was clenching it, and there was no reason to clench it now. It was like walking around with a cocked gun. It was only then that he realized his mistake, and it had nothing to do with the fist he was making. It was about what was inside the fist.

The swan. As he'd left the girl in the closet, he'd never moved the swan to his pocket. There was probably nothing left of it but crushed glass, since he'd smashed Johnny Two Pair with that same fist, but it didn't matter. If Nick saw the glass, it would raise questions.

"Oh, yeah, sorry," he said. He relaxed his grip just a little—not so much that the swan spilled out, but hopefully enough to fool Nick—and shifted his arm a little behind his thigh. "Guess I'm just kind of jacked up, you know?"

Nick wasn't fooled. If anything, Goon had probably made it worse. Nick was still smiling, but his eyes changed. Sometimes they looked blue, but mostly they looked gray. Now they looked solid black.

"You got something in your hand, pal?"

"What's that?"

Now Nick's smile faded. He took his hand off the knob. "I asked you a question, Glen. What's in your hand?"

There was no way around it now. Goon raised his right hand and opened his fingers, palm up. Miraculously, the swan was unharmed. If anything, it looked even more beautiful than before, a tiny angel of light.

Nick frowned. "You stole a glass swan?"

"I like it. Johnny Two Pair won't need it no more."

"Shit, man."

"I know. I'm sorry, boss."

Nick sighed. Goon made sure to wear his best hangdog look, a real Lennie masterpiece that Goon still practiced from time to time in the mirror. As long as Nick went on believing that Goon was dumber than him, then Nick wouldn't be afraid of him, and that was a good thing, because scared people were stupid people.

Once again, Nick grabbed the knob. He started to turn it, then stopped. He looked at Goon with his eyebrows raised.

"Did you hear that?" he said.

"What?"

"I thought I heard a noise," Nick said. "From the back."

<hr>

THEY WERE in the dog days of August, or so the weatherman on channel five cheerfully explained on the ten o'clock news while Glen was gathering up his dirty laundry in his Brooklyn flat. He didn't understand why the guy was so cheerful. The more extreme the weather, the more cheerful he got—which, okay, fine, everybody had their thing, but you had to draw the line somewhere. It wasn't right to be cheerful when the old and the infirm in crappy apartments that lacked air conditioning were dying. Someone needed to have a word with the guy. Someone needed to explain that context mattered.

And why did they call it the *dog days* of August, anyway? No dog was dumb enough to be out in hellfire like this. Only people did that, and not many of those either. Just guys like Glen. A guy who had a place to be, a place to be at 10 o'clock on Tuesday nights that he hadn't missed for five months straight —except that one time back in June, and that was because of a job. A job for Goon, not Glen. All the jobs were for Goon. The only time he got to be Glen, *really* be Glen, was on Tuesday nights.

The sky may have been dark, with just a faint

splash of crimson remaining over the brownstones, but there was no wind to bring relief from the heat radiating up from the sidewalk. It was so hot his brains boiled in his skull like a pot roast in a crockpot. He could barely maintain a coherent thought, and today it was vitally important that all his thoughts be coherent.

Because today was the day that Glen was finally going to ask Maggie out on a date.

It was barely cooler in the laundromat, even with air conditioning. It didn't help that the place was packed, way more packed than it had ever been this late on a Tuesday, lots of the aforementioned poor and infirm, making the place stink of sweat, perfume, musty clothes, various foods, and of course detergent and bleach. It surprised him until he realized the obvious: Spending an evening washing your undies, even in a balmy pit, was better than dying in a sweltering apartment.

There were so many people that he assumed all the yellow plastic chairs were filled, but he spotted one near where he usually sat. Then, when a burly guy with a walrus mustache leaned back, he saw Maggie sitting next to the empty seat, smiling and beckoning. Strands of brown hair stuck to her glistening forehead. It made him think of the first time he'd laid eyes on her, when her hair stuck to her forehead because of the rain.

There was something different about her, but he couldn't say what. On his way there, people parted in their usual fashion, like mice fleeing an elephant. Her skimpy white tank top showed off her stunning shoulders to great effect. There was nothing about her that wasn't stunning. He was pleased to see that her most recent bruise, the one on her chin, was almost gone.

"I saved a seat for you," she said, smiling.

That was promising. She'd never said that before. Of course, she'd never shown up before him either. Did it mean something? Her laundry basket full of clothes sat on the ground in front of her, all dirty, so she obviously hadn't been there long. He squeezed in between her and a little gray-haired woman, a woman who was frowning when he came in and frowned even deeper when he sat. He didn't blame her. Nobody wanted to sit next to an elephant.

"How'd you know I'd show up?" he asked.

Maggie arched an eyebrow at him.

"Right," he said. "Because I *always* show up."

She smiled knowingly. It drove him crazy, that smile. She leaned in closer, and the feel of her breath on his cheek made him even crazier. "I had to fight off two old Cuban women who didn't speak a word of English," she said, "plus an Italian baker who tried to buy me off with biscotti, but I kept them all at bay."

He swallowed. "That's impressive."

"And you didn't even smell the biscotti. It was amazing."

"No doubt."

She nodded to the tattered hardcover under his arm. "What's today's reading pleasure?"

He let her read the spine. No need for a fake jacket anymore.

"*A Tale of Two Cities,*" she said. "I've never actually read that one."

"Really? I thought you said you'd read all of Charles Dickens."

"I said I really *like* Charles Dickens. I didn't say I read all of them. *Oliver Twist, Great Expectations*—oh, *A Christmas Carol,* of course. My mom read that one to me." She nodded toward the book again. "What's it about?"

"Well, it's, um, a historical novel set in London around the time of the French revolution. This doctor, Manette, he's imprisoned in the French Bastille for eighteen years, and, um, it's also about two guys that . . . that, uh . . . fall in love with his daughter. It's, um, about self-sacrifice, starting over, hope … It's, uh, it's a very good book."

"Are you all right?"

"What?"

"You just seem a little … off. You almost never sound this way when you talk about books. Your whole face just lights up."

He shrugged. "Probably just the heat getting to me."

"Yeah, it's really hot, isn't it?"

They said nothing, looking into each other's eyes.

Ask her, he thought. Right now. Ask her out. This is the moment.

"Your hair," he said.

"What?"

"I was thinking you look different somehow. You cut your hair. It's, um, shorter." Boy, that was a winner. He was really muffing this. "It's pretty. I like it."

She touched the hair over her ear self-consciously. "You think so? It's kind of a mess right now."

"No, no, it looks real good." Jesus. What was he, twelve? Time to man up. It was either now or he should forget this whole thing. He looked down at the book, the green cloth cover slick with his sweat. "So Maggie—"

"I have news," she said, at the same time.

They looked at each other. There may have been a three-ring circus going on inside the laundromat, but at that moment it was just the two of them.

"Oh, go ahead," she said.

"No, you," he said.

"Oh. Right." She looked down, fidgeting with a wrinkled paperback she held in her lap. He admonished himself for not commenting on it. Stupid. It was Cormac McCarthy's book, *The Road*. He'd never read it. He'd read *Blood Meridian*, a book that he didn't understand yet bizarrely still liked, but not that one. Maybe she could read it to him. Maybe later, much later, weeks, months, he wouldn't rush things, she could even read it to him in bed. All this went through his mind in the few seconds she was fidgeting with the book. "Well," she said, "I was just going to say I have news."

"Oh?"

"It's about Eddie."

"Oh."

She looked up at him. "I know you don't like it when I talk about him, but I think this will make you happy."

"I don't mind it when you talk about him," he said.

She raised her eyebrows in that way of hers.

"Okay," he admitted, "I don't like it when you talk about him."

"That's better. I like it when you're honest."

"I'm honest," he insisted.

She didn't answer this, but he saw the way she wrinkled her nose, and it killed him inside. Was he really that transparent? How much did she know?

"I just ... I just wanted to tell you that Eddie's gone," she said. "For good, I think. He wrote me an email. He said he was taking off for Panama. There's a guy he knows down there that wants help building a house, and they need a decent bricklayer who will work under the table. He told me he doesn't expect to come back ... and ... and to have a good life."

"Oh," Glen said.

"I thought it was bullshit, but it's been five days. I think he's really gone."

"Wow."

"Yeah."

She was choking up, having a hard time getting it out. That surprised him. It irritated him too.

"Well," he said, "now you can get that fresh start you've been talking about. That's a good thing, right?"

She was still fidgeting with her book, not looking at him. "I know it's crazy," she said, "and I know I'm stupid for feeling this way … but I still sort of love him. Jesus. What's wrong with me?"

"Nothing," he said. "Nothing's wrong with you."

"I'm a total fucking disaster."

"No, you're not. You're perfect."

She laughed sharply. Maybe she thought it was a joke, but when she looked at him her smile froze. It was the closest he'd ever come to telling her how he really felt. Asking her out on a date wouldn't be much farther to go. He just had to do it. Her eyes were wide and dark, so unfathomably wide and dark. He was falling right into those eyes.

"Can I ask you something, Glen?"

His throat felt like it was filled with concrete, it was so hard to swallow. Every time she said his name, his real name, it was like she was saying *I love you.* Was she going to beat him to the punch? Now that her loser boyfriend was out of the picture, what was stopping her?

"Sure," he said.

"You got any dreams, Glen?"

"What?"

"I was just thinking. I've talked a lot about my

dreams, getting a fresh start, maybe going to college, doing something more than waiting tables, having a family someday, but you never talk about your dreams. I've asked you before and you just sort of ... I don't know, laugh it off. Say stuff about having the dream of a good cell phone plan. That sort of thing. But I really want to know. What are your dreams? What do you want out of life?"

He was speechless. It was not at all what he expected her to say, but then, maybe it was. Maybe this *was* her way of asking him out, because she was trying to get a sense of him, the real him, the one he'd kept from her. He found himself staring at her upper lip, the way it was greased with sweat. All around them, machines roared and whirred, the chatter of at least a dozen different languages bounced off metal and plastic and tile, and all the while he kept looking at her lip.

Their unwashed laundry still lay at their feet, hers in a basket, his in a white cloth bag. Machines had surely opened up, and yet there was their dirty laundry, still at their feet. He wanted to tell her the truth, but it felt as if he'd be dumping all of his dirty laundry on top of her head. But he was going to do it. He'd always been Glen with her, not Goon, and he wanted to go on being Glen. Glen had a chance with her. Maybe not a big chance, but a chance.

"Well," he began.

And then he realized that if he told her the truth about who he was, and what he did and had done—

all the many, many terrible things he had done—then she would surely guess that her boyfriend probably hadn't run off to Panama after all. She might suspect that Goon had something to do with Eddie's disappearance, and she'd be right. Eddie was never going to hurt her again. That was when it occurred to him that he would never escape Goon. Yes, he was George, but he was also Lennie, and he would always be both. You could not escape who you were. Could he live a life as Glen and keep Goon bottled up inside forever? That was the question.

Then his phone rang.

It was Nick. He knew by the chime. And there was only one reason that Nick would call him this late on a Tuesday night. It would be about a job.

"I gotta go," he said.

<hr>

"You hear that?" Nick said.

Goon felt something cold slide into the pit of his stomach. "I don't hear nothing," he said hurriedly, "maybe it's just—"

"Shh. Listen. Yeah, it's somebody crying—back in one of the rooms."

Of course Goon heard the crying too. The sound was hard to miss, because Adele had stopped playing and it was so quiet that they probably could have heard a spider crawling along the ceiling way back in Johnny Two Pair's massive shoe emporium. If they'd been in Goon's flat, with the ceaseless street noise and the constant bickering neighbors, there was no way they would have heard a spider or anything else that far from the front door. But it wasn't a spider, and this was no noisy Brooklyn neighborhood. It was a silent penthouse suite thirty stories up, with a scared little girl hiding in a closet, a girl who just couldn't keep her fears contained any longer.

Nick started down the hall, his deadly Ruger leading the way. Goon could see it all playing out in front of him, Nick finding the girl, Nick shooting the girl, and yet he felt powerless to do anything but follow his boss like some dumb hulking beast.

Because this wasn't just his boss. This was Nick. This was his brother. More than his brother, really. Goon had never known his father, the guy had probably just been another nameless, drunken one-night stand, and so he had no concept of what a father was, or how they should act. But without Nick, there was no way Goon would have made it in the world. His mother may have taught him to read, the only good thing she ever did for him, but Nick had taught him everything else.

So he followed. He followed, praying for a miracle, not being able to bear the thought of the sweet little thing in the closet, the one who'd given him the glass swan, taking her last breath in front of him. He lumbered along, all Goon and no Glen, all Lennie and no George.

The George part of his personality was hiding in a

dark closet of its own, somewhere in the recesses of his mind. George. Glen. What difference did a name make? It was all just fiction, wasn't it? Yet he knew the truth. He knew if he didn't act, part of him, the better part, would stay hidden in the closet forever. He would always be Goon and nothing more.

Then Nick, following the girl's cries, was creeping into the spare bedroom. Then Nick, with his Ruger at the ready, was opening the closet door. Then Nick was down on his knees, pawing at the shoes until he'd exposed the pretty girl with the curly red hair, the green eyes, and the freckled skin, the girl now trying to shrink into her pink shirt and denim shorts the same way she'd tried to disappear into the shoes. If only she *could* disappear. Just like in a fairy tale, she could disappear, and then it would end like Goon's favorite stories, where the good ones always got away in the end.

"Well, hello sweetheart," Nick said.

And Goon knew. He knew just by the tone of Nick's voice that the girl wasn't going to get any kind of fairy tale ending. Yes, she needed a miracle, but there was only one way she was going to get it.

***

IT TOOK a long time for Maggie to come to the door. Glen was about to knock for a second time, louder, when the chain finally rattled, the deadbolt turned, and there she was, rubbing her eyes and blinking out at him. She wore a pink terry cloth robe the same color as the girl's shirt. Maybe that was a good sign. Maybe it was also a good sign that Maggie felt safe enough with him to open her door in her robe at midnight, with what looked like nothing but a frilly white nightie underneath. He hoped so. He needed all the good signs he could get.

"Glen?" she said.

"Can we come in?"

We. That word must have snapped her awake, because she really focused on the redheaded girl he was holding in his arms, the girl who shivered and pressed herself against his leather jacket. It might have been early September, but the breeze had Fall's chill bite, and the overhanging oaks, lit up from the porch lights lining the concrete walkway, were already bursting with red and yellow leaves. Changing seasons. It didn't always happen according to schedule.

"What's going on?" Maggie asked.

"We don't have a lot of time. This girl's in danger."

"What?"

"Please, Maggie."

She looked more confused than skeptical, but then the girl started to cry, and Maggie ushered them into her apartment. It smelled of lasagna. It was a tiny place, decorated with chipping Ikea furniture and thrift store cast offs, and it felt even smaller because there were books everywhere: packing cheap particle board shelves, piled on end tables, and perched precariously everywhere else. It was exactly as Glen had pictured it would be.

"It's okay, honey," Maggie said, patting the girl's hair. "It's okay. You're safe here." She looked up at Glen. "What's her name?"

"I don't know," he said.

"You don't know her name? What did you do, kidnap her?"

She chuckled, but the laughter died when she looked into his eyes. That was when Glen realized just how insane his plan would seem to Maggie. He didn't even know the girl's name. He actually didn't even know if she could speak; she hadn't said a word since he'd carried her out of Johnny Two Pair's penthouse and down to Nick's Cadillac. It looked bad.

Then the girl surprised them both.

"Anna," she said, between sniffles. "My name's Anna. Please … please don't make me go back to the bad man. I want to stay with you. *Please.*"

That got Maggie to tear up. "Oh sweetie," she said, rubbing the girl's back again. Then, to Glen: "What's going on? Tell me."

"It's better if I tell you on the road. Do you still have your ex's old Mazda truck? Get dressed and—"

"Glen, I'm not going anywhere until you tell me what's going on. I'm serious."

She crossed her arms and stared at him. Far from being put off by it, he liked the defiance. He hadn't seen much fierceness from her before, and it was a good thing. He turned toward the door, thinking about the Cadillac parked three blocks away. Even if Milo was already looking for him, they wouldn't come here. They wouldn't know about Maggie. Yet.

It was more the next part of the plan that made him feel desperate to get going. But this was his moment of truth with Maggie, where he had to lay it all bare. He hadn't wanted to do it like this, but there was no escaping it now.

"There's a lot I want to tell you," he said, "but I need to make it fast, okay? If you decide to come with me, I'll answer any questions you have, but right now I'm just going to give you the bare bones version."

"Come with you?" she said.

"Just listen. I'm not just a bouncer at the Corner Pocket. I'm a sort of … an enforcer for an organization. Basically the Russian mafia, okay? And my partner, Nick, he's a hitman. On a job tonight, I found this girl, and Nick was going to … well, I had to stop him. Otherwise something bad might happen to her, you get my drift?"

"Oh," Maggie said, her right hand fluttering to her throat. "Is your partner, is he …?"

"He's alive. I knocked him out, then I found some duct tape and tied him up. I don't know how much time we have, but … I have to go on the run with— with Anna, here. I've been preparing for this moment for years. I have almost a hundred grand in cash back at my place, plus some fake passports that will allow us to have a fresh start. I know it seems nuts, and I expect you to say no, but I want you to come with me."

She looked at him for a long time, her eyes wide, her mouth parted. It might have only been a few seconds, but it was long enough that he heard a dog barking on the other side of the complex, the low hum of her refrigerator, and his own ragged breathing.

"Wow," she said.

It wasn't a no. It wasn't a yes either, but he was encouraged that it wasn't a flat refusal. Now came the rest, the part he'd been rehearsing for months.

"I know I'm a bad man, Maggie," he said. "I'm a thug and I'm no good. But I want to be different. I want a second chance. I want it with *you,* but I've been too scared to tell you any of this. You asked me about my dreams. I have dreams. I do. I'd like to get a little place in the woods out west. Maybe near Ashland, where they have the Oregon Shakespeare Festival. We could read a lot of books. Make sure Anna has a good life. I'd keep you both safe. I know— I know I'm not much to look at, but I'd never hurt you, and I'd stay with you as long as you want me."

She teared up, and though the tears didn't fall, they were very close. "Oh Glen," she said.

"Do you believe me?"

"Yes. I knew you were more than a bouncer at that bar. And I heard stories about who owns it. I kind of figured. And … well, you're not the only one who did some Googling, you know."

"What?"

"You found out where I lived, didn't you?"

He felt himself blushing at that. Blushing like a schoolgirl, and that's how he felt, like a silly schoolgirl harboring a silly schoolgirl fantasy. Now that he'd said it all aloud, he could see how stupid it was. Of course it wasn't going to happen. Of course she'd never run off with him. What had he been *thinking?*

"I'm sorry," he said, trying to think of some way to extricate himself without upsetting her any further. "It's a little stalker-like, isn't it? I shouldn't have done it. I should have just asked you out on a proper—"

"Wait a second," she said. "You said you have passports, as in plural."

"Yeah, one for both of us. New identities to start over."

"You got me a fake passport?"

"Oh, trust me, it's real enough."

Now she really did start to cry. "Jesus. That's like the most romantic thing anyone's ever done for me. Of course I'll go with you."

Then she did something he'd been dreaming about since the first moment she walked into the laundromat.

She kissed him.

THE MAZDA GRINDED and groaned the whole way to Glen's place, spitting out massive clouds of black smoke, but it was all right. They only needed it to get to Newark, where they'd dump the truck and hop an Amtrak to Baltimore. There, Glen would buy another car with cash—he knew a guy who would help him—and then they'd drive to Oregon.

It was almost two in the morning by the time he finally parked at the curb down the street from his place—after two drive-bys. He didn't spot anyone from the organization. His flat, on the second floor of a brick building on a narrow street lined with brick buildings, was dark. The three of them sat hip to hip in the cramped cab, Glen driving, Anna in the middle, Maggie on the right. She had a suitcase sandwiched between her legs and a backpack clutched in her arms. She was dressed in jeans and the same gray sweatshirt as when he first met her.

He killed the engine, praying it would start back up again in a few minutes. Using his rearview mirror, he watched his place for a while, saw nothing, then handed Maggie the keys. The wide canopy of the maple tree next to the truck blocked the streetlamp and cast her face in shadow.

"I'll be back before you know it," he said.

"Why are you giving me the keys?" she said.

"Just in case," he said.

She looked up at his flat, then back at him, the fear palpable. "I thought you said your partner's all tied up?"

"He is."

"Then why—?"

"If I'm not back in fifteen minutes, you book it out of here, you understand?"

"Glen—"

"It's going to be okay, Maggie. Listen, I don't think anybody will find Nick until morning. I'll put in an anonymous call to the police once we're safely away, and that should do it. They'll lock him up for killing Johnny Two Pair. But the people we work for, they won't let me walk. They just won't. And he's going to tell them about the girl. They'll find her. So we have to start over. We need the passports and the cash. It's the only way."

"What about her parents?" Maggie asked.

"They died," Anna said.

"Oh, sweetie, I'm so sorry. Do you have other relatives?"

"I don't know," she said. "I want—I want to stay with you."

Maggie looked at him. He shrugged.

"We'll figure it out," he said. "Let's just get to Oregon first."

Before she could slow him down with more questions, he hopped out of the truck. The night was colder than it had any right to be. The grass, cordoned off from the sidewalks behind low brick walls and decorative cast iron fencing, was even glazed with white. There was no one around, which was the important thing. He started for the double glass doors that led to his lobby, then realized he was still cupping the glass swan in his gloved hand. All this time. Crazy.

He returned to the truck and motioned for Maggie to roll down the window, which she did.

"Here," he said, trying to hand the swan to the girl. "You hold onto this for me, okay?"

Anna shook her head. "It's a good luck charm. It'll keep you safe."

She looked like she might launch into hysterics if he pushed it, so he nodded and headed for his building. His heart boomed in his ears. It was funny. Usually he was cool under pressure, maybe not as cool as Nick, but he'd long since gotten past any real nerves on a job. But this wasn't a job, was it? Now, despite the chill, his collar was damp and his shirt stuck to his back.

As impatient as he felt to get on the road, he forced himself to take his time as he passed through the deserted lobby and took the back stairwell to his floor. Someone down the hall of beige doors—probably old Bo Anderson, an insomniac—was watching television, but otherwise it was still. His door was locked. Good. Standing off to the side, he unlocked it and swung it open into darkness. Nobody fired any shots. His refrigerator hummed. His dehumidifier whirred. No other sounds.

He waited for a count of five, holding his breath, then reached in and flicked on the entry light. He peered around the door frame and saw no one inside.

His place wasn't much bigger than Maggie's, but

the furniture was much nicer—a smoked glass coffee table, a black leather couch and loveseat, and a plush white rug that covered most of the walnut floor, none of which he'd picked out himself. That had all been Nick. It smelled of the bacon and eggs he'd had for breakfast, a lifetime ago.

The first thing he did was go to the window, cracking open the blinds to make sure Maggie and Annie were still out in the truck. They were. He set the glass swan on the windowsill—he didn't know why he did this, it would have been better to put it in his pocket—then headed for the mahogany bookshelf behind the couch. It was the one thing that really *was* him, ironically enough, or at least partly so. It was bursting with books, half of which were crap celebrity biographies he pretended to read, half of which were stuff he actually *did* read, but he'd covered this by telling Nick he owned some books just for their color. Dumb old Goon, just picking books for show. Nick bought it completely.

He took off his gloves and tossed them aside, then squatted on his haunches and pulled out the big Webster's dictionary. Nick would have been suspicious if Glen had a safe, but fake books with false interiors did the trick well enough. He opened it and pulled out the two passports.

The bottom row was a set of Harvard Classics, green boards with gold gilt spines. He removed the middle five books. Each was filled with rubber-banded stacks of cash—twenty in all, in various denominations, though mostly hundreds. Ninety-two thousand dollars, the last he'd counted.

He was stuffing these into the various pockets of his leather jacket when somebody spoke.

"Goon."

The hairs on the back of his neck rose. Nick. Glen knew the voice. He knew it even though Nick seldom called him Goon, and he certainly never called him Goon like that, like it was an insult, like he couldn't spit out the word fast enough. Glen didn't move.

"But you were never Goon to *me*," Nick said. "You were always my brother. And this is how you treat your brother?"

Glen knew by the direction of the voice that Nick was standing in the doorway to the bathroom. That meant he'd been here all along, waiting. Glen castigated himself for not checking the whole flat first. And they'd taken way too long at Maggie's. Sloppy, all of it. And now it was going to cost him.

"You got nothing to say for yourself?" Nick said.

"I'm sorry, boss," Glen said, trying to sound contrite, which was hard to do when he was clutching wads of cash. "I'm—I'm really sorry. I don't know what I—"

"*Sorry?* Sorry, my ass. You've got all that money squirreled away and you tell me you're sorry? And passports too. Shit. You been planning this forever. You know how much I defended you to Milo? And you do *this?*"

"I know, I just—"

"Shut up! Just shut the fuck up. You say one more thing, I swear I'm going to call Milo and tell him everything. Now stand up and turn around. Slow. No stupid shit. You done enough stupid shit tonight as it is."

Glen felt the first glimmer of hope. So Nick hadn't called Milo. That meant it could still play out all right—maybe not for him, but for Maggie and Anna, at least. Nick didn't know about them in the truck. If Glen stalled long enough, Maggie would leave. She might not have the cash or the passports, but she'd at least have a chance.

"You hear me, Goon?" Nick said. "I told you to get your ass up! Or you deaf now as well as dumb? That's what I'm calling you, you know. It's Goon here on out. It's all you deserve. Now stand up and keep your hands where I can see them."

Glen stood, raising his arms. Slow. Everything had to be slow. All Maggie and Anna needed was time.

"Turn around!" Nick said.

Glen did, but with all the speed of a drunken tortoise, keeping his head sunk low. Sheepish. Ashamed. How much time had passed since he'd left Maggie? Ten minutes? Not nearly enough.

When he finally looked up, Nick was exactly where Glen expected him to be—in the doorway to the bathroom, pointing the Ruger Mark IV with its long suppressor at Glen. That was another mistake on Glen's part. He'd left it by Johnny Two Pair's body, wanting the police to find the murder weapon, but if he'd at least hidden it somewhere in the penthouse, maybe back in the shoe emporium, Nick would have had to get his hands on another piece before coming here. Dumb, so dumb. Goon may have been slow, but Glen could be downright idiotic. It was true what they said. Love could make people stupid.

"You gonna shoot me, boss?" Glen said.

"Depends on you," Nick said. "Depends on what happens next."

The bump on Nick's forehead was as big as a cue ball, his rigid column of blonde hair dented fully on one side. The dent might have made Glen laugh if the circumstances had been different.

"I said I'm sorry," Glen said, sniffling, really laying the Lennie act on thick. "I really am."

"Where's the little girl?"

"I dropped her off at the police station."

"Bullshit."

"I just couldn't kill her, boss. I'm sorry."

"If you was just gonna drop her off, then why you got two passports?"

Glen swallowed. "It's for this lady," he said. "This stripper over at Jugs and Suds. I go there sometimes. Her name's Candy. She's real nice. I was gonna ask her to run away with me. I know it's stupid, but—"

"What's that?" Nick said.

The question wasn't about what Glen was saying, but about what Nick was now looking at. Even as the Ruger was still trained on Glen, Nick was staring at the glass figurine on the windowsill. The way it caught the light, the slender neck glowed as if it had swallowed a tiny star.

"Just the swan," Glen said. "I like it. I know it's dumb, but I like it."

Nick eyed Glen for a long time—still not long enough, not nearly long enough—then walked to the windowsill. The distance between them was almost the entire width of the room, about fifteen feet. Too far to make a play. Nick picked up the swan with his left hand, careful to keep the Ruger pointed at Glen. Time passed. This was good. The more time, the better.

But then Nick cracked open the blinds and peered outside.

"Well, what do you know?" he said. "There's our little girl now, sitting pretty as can be in that truck, looking right at me. And is that your stripper friend in the driver seat?"

Glen felt as if he stood at the mouth of a tunnel, the light on the other side shrinking until it was just a dot. Even if Maggie left now, her odds of escaping had gone down dramatically. Whether Nick could read the license number from here or not, there were only so many Mazda trucks still on the road, especially ones that looked like that. Once Nick got the passports, he'd figure out who Maggie was by her picture. It wouldn't take him long, not with the resources of the organization.

No, the only hope Maggie and Anna had now

rested with Glen. He had to get the jump on Nick. It was too far, way too far, but there was no other way. At least Nick was looking out the window, not at him, and the Ruger, while still pointed at Glen, had dipped ever so slightly.

Glen tensed his fists, preparing to charge.

"Don't do it, man," Nick said, the Ruger once again leveled and steady as if by magic. "I'll put three slugs in the middle of your chest before you even take a step."

And he would too. There was no doubt about that. Nick turned and faced him, the Ruger like an extension of his right hand, the glass swan pinched between the thumb and forefinger of his left.

"You made a mistake," Nick said. "I'm gonna cover for you, like always, but you gotta make it right. We're going to go down to that old truck and take care of things. You know what you gotta do. You do that, and give me that money there as payment for what you done to me, and we'll call it square. Milo don't have to know."

Glen hesitated. Nick was not a good man. Glen was not a good man either, but there was still hope for him, just an ember of hope, maybe, but hope nonetheless. Nick, however, was rotten to the core. There was no saving him. He could kill a little girl one minute and turn right around and buy popcorn at Coney Island the next. He wouldn't feel any remorse.

And yet, despite all this, Glen loved Nick. It

wasn't just because he owed Nick. He really did care about him. Deep down, Glen suspected there was only one way this could go, but he owed it to Nick to give him another option.

"You hear me, dumbass?" Nick said. "I told you how this is going to play out, so give me the cash and we can get to it before your stripper friend gets any silly ideas in her head."

"No," Glen said. "That's not how this is going to play out, Nick. Here's what you're going to do. You're going to put down the gun, I'm going to tie you up again, much better this time, and then I'm going to walk out of here."

Nick laughed. Glen didn't.

"I'm serious," Glen said. "I don't want to hurt you. You really have been like a brother to me—like a father, really, but I have to leave now. I'm not going back to my old life. I've made my decision."

"What's up with your voice?" Nick said. "You sound different."

"I *am* different. Or maybe I'm just the me I always was and now you finally see it. Put down the gun."

"What're you doing?" Nick said. "I told you not to take a step."

"My hands are up, Nick. If you shoot me, you're doing it in cold blood."

"Don't."

"I just want to tie you up, that's all. Nobody has to get hurt."

"*You're* going to get hurt, if you keep coming."

"I won't even punch you, if you just put down the gun."

"Don't. Man, don't do this."

And yet, Glen did—one more shuffling step, not wanting to give Nick any reason to pull the trigger just out of instinct. The problem was the distance. Fifteen feet was too much. He needed to get it down to ten. Then, even if Nick fired, he might have a chance. He was a thug, after all. There was a lot to him. He could probably take a few bullets.

Another step. Nick started to cry, big ugly tears. That was a first. Glen had never seen Nick cry before, and it gave Glen a momentary pause, not because he was having second thoughts, but because he knew that the tears meant Nick was going to shoot him. Nick was crying because he was already grieving. Glen couldn't let Nick live. Even if Glen managed to survive, he knew with absolute certainty that Nick would never stop coming for him. And if he died? Nick would never stop coming for Maggie and Anna.

Glen was going to have to punch Nick with everything he had. Maybe he would get lucky and survive, maybe Nick would even miss, but Glen couldn't count on it. One punch to kill. That was how it had to go.

"Listen—" Nick said.

But Glen, launching himself at Nick, was beyond listening. His fist, his massive Goon fist, was flying at Nick's face. The Ruger fired—one shot, two, but not three, Glen had prevented that at least by closing the distance, but two shots tore up his insides as his fist made contact with the end of Nick's nose. There wasn't much nose after he hit it, all that power driving the cartridge and bone back into Nick's brain as surely as any bullet.

Then Nick was falling backward, the Ruger flinging in one direction, the swan in the other. Glen, his gut on fire, kept moving forward. The swan was in the air. It was soaring through the air and it was spinning. Glen, already tasting blood in his mouth, reached for it.

He was going down, following Nick to the floor, but he was reaching for the swan with his right hand.

His bare hand.

No gloves.

Just his big ugly thug hand and big ugly thug fingers, grasping for the most precious thing he had ever owned.

THE MAZDA WAS STILL at the curb, the engine silent, the cab fogged up with the warm breath of the two people inside. Even with his leather jacket zipped up tight, it felt chillier to Glen than before. Considering everything that had just gone down in his flat, the neighborhood was strangely silent. It wouldn't be that way for long.

"Oh, thank God," Maggie said, when he leaned down to the open window.

"You didn't listen to me," he said.

"I know, I know, but I just couldn't leave you. Get in. We can switch later."

She was in the driver's seat, and maybe it was because she was looking across the cab that she didn't take note of his appearance, but Anna was not fooled.

"You got blood on your lips," she said.

"Yeah," Glen said.

"What?" Maggie said. "Glen, what's happened? Why are you holding your stomach like that? Glen—"

"Stay calm," he said. "You're —you're going to need to stay calm. Here, everything you need is inside."

He placed the paper sack, which now contained the cash, Maggie's passport, and the glass swan, on the seat next to Anna. The girl started to cry. So did Maggie.

"What're you doing?" Maggie said.

"You … need to go," he said.

"No. Not without you."

He coughed and more blood speckled his hand. "It's the only way. With me out of the picture, you … you have a chance. And I won't last an hour anyway."

"No!" Maggie insisted. "We can go to a hospital. We can—"

"Maggie, please."

She shook her head, about to say something else,

but then sirens rose up in the distance. She looked at him with alarm.

"Yeah, I called them," he said.

"Why?"

"To force you to go. They … they might see you as an accessory to murder. Maybe kidnapping. So you gotta … go." He groaned. He was trying to keep the pain bottled up, but it was just too much.

"No," she said.

"Yes. Right now."

Maggie shook her head. The sirens grew louder. Glen teetered on his feet, the night closing in around him, everything going dark. He didn't have much time.

"Don't you see, Maggie?" he said. "I'm a thug. I'm a *goon*. I've done … terrible, terrible things. But I did a good thing here. Don't … ruin it by staying. If I go with you, even if I live, the people I work for—they'll never stop looking for me. But if I die here … they have no reason to follow you. So you gotta go. Dump the Mazda soon, but use the passport. You can—you can probably come back to your old life eventually, but I hope you don't. It's your fresh start. Take it. Go to Oregon. Go to Ashland. Think of me sometimes, but *go*."

She was crying so much she couldn't speak. He patted Anna on the head, who was crying too, then reached across the cab and touched Maggie's shoulder. She grasped at his bloody fingers, trying to hold him, but he managed to extricate himself and walk away.

It was the hardest thing he'd ever done. The sirens were so loud he couldn't hear the crying behind him, so loud he could barely make out the Mazda's engine sputtering to life.

He was trying to make it to the lobby of his building, but he had to settle for the curb. He sat, watching the red glow of Mazda taillights disappear around the corner even as blue light pulsed on all the brick facades at the other end of the street. All around him, bedroom lights flickered on. Windows opened. Faces. Voices.

He was clutching his side with his fist, his closed fist, and he realized that he was holding something. He opened his bloody fingers and there was the swan. He still had it in his hand. It was streaked with blood, but the glass still sparkled. What a funny thing. He distinctly remembered putting the swan in the paper sack.

Then Goon, staring off in the direction the Mazda had gone, realized that the swan *was* in the paper sack. Glen had it. Glen was in the truck and the swan was with him. This was Goon's swan, for him to hold at the very end, and so hold it he did. As the police cruiser screeched to a halt inches from his outstretched legs, he looked down at the swan and kept its brilliance, its lovely curves, its brilliant light, fixed in his mind even as the world went dark around him for the final time.

THERE WAS ENOUGH OF HER

THE ALIEN SHIP landed in the Oak Hill Elementary parking lot at 11:39 a.m. The time would be recorded by the security cameras mounted on the school, as well as the ones at Rexton Car Wash just up the road, but Mary Lee Stuggart noted it because she happened to glance at the clock above the window. She'd wanted to know how much time she had before the lunch bell—six minutes—and instead she saw a Martian climbing out of a blocky green and brown spaceship almost perfectly camouflaged with the arbor vitae bushes at the back of the lot.

Six minutes. A lot could happen in six minutes.

She didn't know it was a Martian, of course. It could have been from Venus, Jupiter, or who knew where, but the bulky, black, bug-eyed creature lumbering her way *seemed* like it was from Mars. Besides, Larry was always going on about how if the aliens *did* visit, they'd be from a nearby planet, since nothing could travel faster than the speed of light and everything was so far apart in space. Mary didn't know what the speed of light had to do with anything, but she did know Mars was close and this alien had come in a small ship.

It was the last Friday in May—sunny, blue skies, the grass still lush as it always was this time of year in the Willamette Valley. No wonder the alien had chosen today for his visit. Even the dappled shade from the Oregon white oaks, on the few cars out there, looked magical. It was the kind of day that when people from California visited, they said, "Hey hon, it's like home but greener, so let's move," not knowing that the reason it was so green was that it had rained for the past six months.

Five minutes until the lunch bell.

Mary looked back at the board and saw the sentence she'd just written in white chalk: "The <u>cat</u> ran up the <u>tree</u>." She didn't know why the words "cat" and "tree" were underlined. She knew a moment ago and she didn't know now. It didn't have anything to do with the alien, either. She was always forgetting things these days.

Calm as could be, she put down the chalk and turned to the class, making sure not to look at the window again. If she looked at the window, *they* would look, and she didn't want that. She did it slowly, keeping her hand on the stool she'd positioned there to keep from falling. She was a big woman, after all, bigger than she'd ever been, and it didn't take much for her to lose her balance. And if she fell, there'd be no getting up without a great deal of help and a whole lot of snickering—not just from the kids, either. Even some of the teachers called her old Mrs. Slug Fart behind her back. She may have been forgetful, but her hearing was just fine.

"Let's—let's have story time, class," Mary said. "In the cozy corner, like always."

The children looked confused. They were still staring at her, not the window, thank God. The alien was moving slowly, but he was definitely coming their way, and he had some kind of metal pincer attached to his arm. That pincer would scare the living daylights out of these kids. She'd only taught first graders for three years, but she knew they frightened easily. Now, the fourth graders she'd taught for twenty-five years before Principal Meyers forced her to change, saying the parents had "concerns," whatever that meant, they were a different matter. Deep down, the fourth graders were usually *more* scared than the first graders, since they knew more about the world, maybe even that aliens could be real, but they could at least put on a brave front. They could pretend. Sometimes pretending to be brave was all you needed.

Four minutes.

Most of the time, Mary pretended to be brave, even if she didn't feel it. Even if she almost never felt it. She'd had to pretend ever since she was a little girl, when everybody made fun of her because of her size, and Daddy always told her to be brave and not let people know the teasing got to her. Fatso. Chubby girl. Lard butt. She'd heard it all. She'd certainly pretended to be brave the last few years as she struggled to keep it together—not just for herself, she never cared all that much about herself, but for Larry, she had to keep it together for Larry. He needed her. He'd already lost one leg to the diabetes and he might lose another. Two years before she was eligible for full retirement. She could make it two years. His disability income just wasn't going to cut it.

She might have been a big woman, but there was another way to look at it too. She always told herself that she was big because she had to be. There was enough of her. There had to be enough of her—to shoulder the load, to take on people's problems, to make life easier for everybody. Didn't she do it for Larry? Hadn't she done it for her mother, when she still lived with them? And for Lexi, who'd had that lisp growing up, but look at her now, being brave herself at the University of Oregon in Eugene.

"But it's almost lunch time, ma'am," Jimmy Blackburn said. He was a good kid. Always said ma'am. Nobody said ma'am anymore. She was pretty sure he never had enough to eat at home, since she often caught him rifling through kids' lunches in the coat room behind the cozy corner, but that didn't make him bad. Just hungry. "I mean, there's like—"

"No backtalk now! Hurry up, everyone! Huddle

real close. My—my voice is still kinda getting over that cold, so I might need to whisper."

Being a sensitive kid, Jimmy teared up, and she felt bad about that, but there was just no time for the usual back and forth. Blonde-haired, pigtailed Emma Whistler, who always wanted to be first at everything, sprang up and rushed to the cozy corner, and then the rest of the kids followed suit. Mary glanced at the window and saw the alien was heading for the north side door, the one that was supposed to be locked but often wasn't because the instructional aid, Travis, wanted to get back inside after sneaking a smoke. He was hardly more than a kid himself and could be a real bonehead, but she liked Travis anyway. She would have liked him even if he hadn't treated her like a regular person, but she liked him even more because of it.

Three minutes.

She turned toward the blackboard, away from the kids, using her wide back to block their view, and reached into the fanny pack that hung below her belly. Because Larry insisted she have a cell phone on her at all times, in case she fell down and nobody was around, she had one in the pack, and she was very glad for it today. Her hand shook as she dialed 9-1-1.

"There's an alien," she said, keeping her voice low. "At Oak Hill Elementary."

"Ma'am?" the dispatcher said.

"An alien!" she said. "Just landed in the parking lot. Send help."

She hung up when he was asking for clarification. The alien was at the north side door, just one classroom away. *It was opening the door.* She saw it clearly. It really was unlocked. That Travis, she loved him even though he was stupid. She turned back to the kids—too fast, darn it—and almost fell, but she didn't black out. The world flickered in and out around her, but she managed to stay on her feet. But when she blinked at the kids, she saw that they all looked scared now. Xavier, Tess, Roberto, Eva. All of them.

"An alien?" Jimmy said.

So they'd heard her. Too bad. "Never—never mind that," she said, shuffling toward them. Be brave, she told herself. One foot in front of the other. Focus. "Hey, I have an idea. Let's do story time in the coat room."

"I just heard someone scream!" Annie said.

"That's—that's just a movie next door, dear," Mary said. "Hustle up everyone, into the coat room. That will be fun. Something different."

Two minutes.

She lumbered her way toward them, more sliding than walking because it was dangerous for her to lift her feet off the tiles, telling herself to be brave. There was enough of her. Two years, two minutes, what was the difference? She could keep it together.

"I heard firecrackers!" Laya said.

Mary shushed her and herded them into the windowless coat room, where it was shadowy and crowded, especially with all the colorful coats and backpacks hung on the hooks. It smelled of plastic, uneaten bananas, and bark chips from the playground. And something else. Pee? Little Desi probably wet her panties again and tried to hide them in her coat. Or maybe one of them had peed right now. The kids could barely fit, their little faces, such babies, looking up at her. A lot of them were crying now.

Mary hated to see them cry. Was that Lexi there in the back? No, Mary was just seeing things again. She had to keep it together. The cat ran up the tree. What was a cat? It didn't matter. An alien had come to Oak Hill Elementary.

One minute.

She heard sirens outside, fast approaching. She heard screaming in the hall. There was no door to the coat room, just an opening, and it was a pretty big opening too. That was okay. Mary Lee Stuggart was a big woman, as big as she had ever been, and she filled the space.

The bell rang. It was lunch time, but they weren't going anywhere. It was the alien who was coming for lunch, to eat the little ones, and Mary wasn't going to allow it. The classroom door banged open. If she turned, she'd see the alien with its big bug eyes and long metal pincer, but she didn't dare look. She put her hands on both sides of the opening and braced herself. No matter what happened, she was never letting go. She could do this. She could be brave.

There was enough of her.

MAKE SURE YOU CALL COLLECT

I MET Tom Gaffin when I was waiting tables at the Denny's on Landon Avenue. It was Super Bowl Sunday, so the restaurant was deserted. It was also deserted because it was raining like crazy outside, a real howler—thunder, lighting, the whole deal.

We got a lot of drizzle in Rexton during the winter months, but real thunderstorms were rare. In between refilling iced teas for two housewives seeking refuge from their football-fanatic husbands, and serving burgers to a pair of pimply, black-clad gamer boys who barely looked up from their phones, I spent most of my shift glancing at the dreary parking lot and worrying about my '77 Corvette.

I'd stupidly parked under one of the only trees in the lot, a sturdy white oak, and yet the massive thing didn't look nearly so sturdy now that I was watching one of its big leafless branches sway violently above my shiny yellow hood. I was so behind on my insurance payments that I doubted they'd pay out, so if the branch broke that would be it for my pretty car. At five to eight, I asked Megs if I could take my break early so I could move it.

She told me to go home instead, since it was too slow for three servers and I was low on the totem pole. I should have been pissed, because I really needed the money, but I was so drained from the screaming match I'd had with Julia yesterday that I didn't put up much of an argument.

That was how I came to be standing between the two glass doors, waiting for at least *some* respite from the deluge, when snowy-haired Tom Gaffin staggered out of the lounge to join me. In restaurant lingo, this was the vestibule, but most of the staff called it the fishbowl, partly because of the glass and how we could ogle the customers as they came in, but also, weirdly, because it smelled like fish. The theory was it had something to do with the adhesive used to put down the orange ceramic tiles, but really, it was anybody's guess. Every restaurant I'd ever worked—most of them back before my law degree, of course—always had its weirdness.

"Well, *sheeeit,*" Tom said.

I chuckled. Even with those two words, I caught a whiff of the gin and tonic on his breath. I knew booze with one sniff like a good florist knows flowers—not that I'm proud of this particular talent, at least not anymore. With his shock of white hair, round face, and ruddy complexion, Tom looked like a beardless Santa Claus. He was dressed in a gray London Fog trench coat over a blue cardigan sweater, dressed to the nines as usual. He stepped up to the glass and cupped his liver-spotted hands over his eyes, peering outside.

At the time, I pegged him as in his late seventies. I found out later I'd overestimated by a decade. That made him roughly the same age my father would have been, if a widowmaker hadn't gotten him eight years ago.

The truth was, Tom had actually been coming to our Denny's for a few months, but I didn't know who he was other than some old rich dude who drove a twenty-year-old Cadillac DeVille and always staggered into the lounge around five o'clock, half-drunk already, then staggered out again at eight o'clock on the nose, which explained how we both ended up in the fishbowl at the same time.

I found out later that the reason he was drinking at our particular Denny's was that he couldn't drink anywhere else. Every other bar in Rexton had banned him for unruly behavior. Maybe that was why he wasn't quite so unruly with us, because he knew there was nowhere else to go.

As he stared into the murk, his breath fogged the glass. "I would have brought my swimming trunks," he said, "if I would have known I was going for a dip. Man, this is never going to end, is it?"

"Yeah," I said, "it's really coming down."

He leaned back from the window to look at me,

listing so much on his feet that his Italian leather wingtips squeaked on the wet tiles. He was decades older than me, but beyond the saggy, wrinkled flesh he had the same bloodshot blue eyes I often saw when I looked in the mirror. "Coming *down?*" he said. "Son, this is God taking a piss after drinking all the Bloody Marys he saved up during Prohibition."

This got another chuckle out of me. I always liked people who could make me laugh—Julia was like that, once upon a time—and when I liked someone, I was predisposed to help them. Which explained what I did next, despite these being the first words we'd shared.

"I'll tell you what, Tom," I said, "how about I give you a ride home? It's no kind of night to be driving if you've been drinking."

He raised his bushy white eyebrows. "You know me?"

"Sure, I do. *Of* you, anyway." I thought about coming up with a fib to explain why—with my windbreaker hiding my black polo and black slacks, he obviously thought I was just a customer—but I knew Tom would figure out the truth soon enough. "I work here," I added. "I'm a waiter."

"Oh!" he said. "Well, now. Sorry I didn't recognize you, son."

"No worries. I'm Jake Conroy, by the way. So what do you say, Tom? Want a lift?"

"Well, that's mighty nice of you, Jake, but I'm sure

I can manage. It's why I always go home at eight on the dot, no matter what. Ronnie's Rules."

"Ronnie?"

He made the sign of the cross. "My wife, God rest her soul."

"Oh, I'm sorry."

"Long time ago now," he said, but the way it came out, his voice pinched and his forehead furrowing, it didn't sound like a long time ago. "She had a lot of rules for me, which I hated at the time, but she knew me best. When I lose my way, it's usually because I forget them."

I didn't really know what to say to this, so I just repeated my offer. Once again, he demurred.

"No, no," he said, "you're a nice boy, but I'll be all right."

"You sure? I'll even pick you up right at the door. You'll barely even get wet. And you can just take an Uber back here tomorrow to get your Cadillac."

He furrowed his big eyebrows again. "Uber?"

"A taxi."

"Oh! What is he, your favorite driver? Sounds Pakistani." He sighed. "All right, but only if we take my ride. You can drive, and I'll give you fifty for your trouble. Oh, hell, I'll make it a hundred so you can call your buddy Uber to bring you back here."

"Honestly, sir, I'd rather drive my Corvette. And the money's not necessary, really. I just want to make sure you get home safe."

This stopped him cold. "That banana yellow beauty over there is yours?" he said.

"Yeah."

"And you work *here?*"

Now it was my turn to sigh. "I didn't steal it, I promise."

"Huh. You just got a lot more interesting, son. All right, fine, we'll do it your way, but I'm not such a Nancy that I can't make a mad dash through the rain. Let's go!"

Thirty seconds later, we were buckled and shivering in our seats, cold water running into my eyes, my hands shaking as I turned the ignition and the Corvette's beautiful eight cylinders roared to life. It was one of the best sounds in the world, no matter how many times I'd heard it before. It was even better than the smell of the leather seats, which never got old either.

Except to tell me his address—he lived in ritzy Oak Heights, which didn't surprise me in the slightest—Tom didn't say much for the first half of the drive. I made one attempt at conversation, asking if he was still working or retired, but he just stared silently out the rain-streaked passenger window at the dark world outside.

After a while, I figured he might have nodded off, which was no problem. I knew how to get to his house without further direction, chiefly because I used to live in Oak Heights myself—though at the bottom of the hill, with the new strivers, and not at the top, where the richest of the rich lived. About the time I was passing the little brick colonial with the white shutters, disappointed that Julia had already closed all the blinds, Tom finally piped up.

"You got kids, Jake?"

I shot him a sharp glance, wondering if he'd followed my interested gaze, but he hadn't looked at me. His breath misted on the passenger side window.

"Yeah," I said, "a daughter."

"How old?"

"Well, she's … five. No, six. Yeah, def—definitely six."

"You sure?"

Now he finally looked at me, his eyes so hooded I couldn't read them, but the disapproval in his voice was obvious. "Not a good sign, Jake. A father should know how old his kids are."

"I knew it," I insisted. "I just had to think about it a second. She's six. She's in first grade. She—she loves knock-knock jokes."

He snorted and went back to staring out the window, leaving me with my face burning. I asked him if he had kids himself, but he didn't answer. I was starting to regret driving him home. We went back to riding in silence, him filling the car with the smell of gin and tonic, me with the scent of pepper-mint Altoids, tires swishing through puddles, the Corvette barely breaking a sweat as we wound our way up through slick streets and overhanging oaks, lots of glimmering shadows and shimmering pools of yellow streetlight.

I knew approximately where he lived because I'd driven up there a few times to ogle at the mansions, but I didn't know the specific mansion until we were almost upon it and I spotted the silver numbers on the brick column to the left of the cast iron gate.

It wasn't just a specific mansion. It was *that* mansion, as in the biggest of the bunch and one of the oldest to boot, with French Revival architecture, a gatehouse bigger by itself than the post-war Sears kit homes down by the river, and a marble fountain in the middle of a wraparound cobblestone driveway that probably cost more than my—*Julia's*—house, which wasn't cheap itself. The fountain was a replica of Rodin's The Thinker. Of course it was.

I knew all of this from memory. Hardly any of it was visible on this dreary night, because the only light came from the single brass lamp above the gatehouse. The mansion, dark and ominous, loomed at the end of the drive.

"*This* is your house?" I said.

"Don't worry, Jake, I didn't steal it."

"Funny. Okay, now I really gotta know. How *did* you get so rich, anyway?"

"I bought Microsoft when it was twenty-two dollars a share."

"Come on, seriously."

"Just pull up over there and enter the code."

He rattled off the numbers and I dutifully did as

instructed, my hands barely getting misted because the gatehouse roof extended over the keypad. The gatehouse was dark inside, nobody there. The few times I'd been by, it had always been empty.

Except for a faint red glow from the stained-glass side windows flanking the front door, the house was also dark, the whole thing looming over us like an ocean liner. He told me to pull right up to the marble steps, which I did. We went for another swim in the dark, getting even more soaked. It was a good thing I went with him because I had to grab his arm when he slipped on a step.

Soon we were under the cover again and he was opening the door. The air that wafted out smelled like it hadn't mingled with the outside world in a long time—stale and stuffy, smelling of plaster and old wood. He started to go in, then, when I didn't follow, looked over his shoulder and raised his eyebrows.

"Aren't you coming?" he asked.

"No, I really should get going."

"Come on, I need to get that hundred. I think I only have fifty on me right now."

"It's really not necess—"

"I insist. Really."

With a shrug, I followed him inside. It was dark except for the glow of a beaded Tiffany lamp on a walnut credenza, but then he flicked a switch and a crystal chandelier fit for a ballroom filled the entryway with dazzling light. The entryway *was* a ballroom, or at least as big as one, with a high cathedral ceiling, massive gold-framed mirrors, life-size Renaissance portraits of dignified people I didn't recognize, a grandfather clock so huge it could have stood in for Big Ben himself, and a sweeping staircase that led up to an even more sweeping balcony. It was like something out of the Gilded Age.

There were cobwebs everywhere, though, and the air was thick with dust. Even the chandelier, the most impressive thing in the room, was only half lit; most of the bulbs were dark. He shuffled across the patterned parquet flooring and swayed his way toward a pair of French doors off to the right. I stayed where I was, hoping he'd just return in a second, but at the doors he looked at me.

"You want to stay for a drink?" he asked, his voice echoing like we were in a cave. "Just a quick one?"

"Oh, I appreciate the offer, Mr. Gaffin—"

"Ha! A minute ago you were calling me Tom, then you see my place and it's Mr. Gaffin. It's almost Pavlovian, isn't it, the need to worship money?"

"What?"

He nodded toward the French doors. "Come on, I've got some hundred-year-old bourbon that'll knock you on your ass."

"I really need to get home. I'm supposed to take Ella to school in the morning."

He nodded. *"Supposed* to take."

"What's that?"

"Just interesting, that you put it that way. Instead

of saying, 'I have to take Ella to school,' you added the word 'supposed.' It's kind of like the word *try.* That's another thing Ronnie warned me about early on in our marriage. If you say something like, 'I'll *try* to make it,' that means you're already weaseling out of it. Either do or don't, you know, that's what Ronnie always said. That and the little green fella from those Space Wars movies. What was his name? Boda. That's right. There is no try."

He chuckled, but my ears were too hot to tell him he was talking about *Yoda,* not Boda, and that movie was *Star Wars*, not Space Wars. "Listen, just because I word it a certain way doesn't mean—"

"Oh, Jake, you're not going to get all *indignant* on me, are you? I mean, come on, you may be able to fool your manager at Denny's with those Altoids, but you're not fooling me."

"What?"

"You're a lush, pal. Just like me. Probably ruined your life too."

My jaw was so tight it was hard to speak. "I don't know what you're talking about," I insisted.

"Oh, really? That's why a waiter making minimum wage plus tips is driving a '67 Corvette?"

I didn't answer, the two of us staring at each other in that sad but spectacular entryway, like two guys on the Titanic after all the women and children had escaped. Who was this rich asshole to give me lessons on how to live my life? Rather than let Tom Gaffin witness my full mastery of the more colorful side of the English language—identifying booze wasn't the only natural talent I had—I just raised my hands in mock defeat and turned to the door.

That probably would have been how it ended, too, what might have been an interesting anecdote but certainly not an event that changed the trajectory of my life, had Tom not spoken up right then.

"Look, I'm sorry," he said. "I don't have many visitors, so I … Well, anyway, if you just come in for a drink, I'll answer your question. I think you'll find it interesting. You might not believe it, but you'll definitely find it interesting."

The intrigue was enough to get me to stop, though my face still felt like it was on fire. "What question?"

"How I got so rich, son. Isn't that what you really want to know?"

I crossed my arms, not wanting to engage with him but not being able to help myself. "Oh, so you didn't buy Microsoft at twenty bucks a share?"

He laughed again. He was doing all the laughing now, because I was all out of laughs. "Oh, no," he said, "that part's true. It's how I *knew* to buy Microsoft that's interesting. Come on, son, I promise I'll behave."

He opened one of the French doors and disappeared into the darkness, leaving the door open for me. A lamp clicked on from within and warm yellow light cast the shadow of the French doors on the hardwood floor. I heard glasses clinking, and yet still

I stood there, not wanting to give him another opportunity to abuse me, but my curiosity was piqued.

The room beyond the French doors was a study of sorts, with mahogany bookshelves, two blue leather wingbacks, and a massive oak desk that looked like something Thomas Jefferson might have owned. There was a decorative flintlock pistol mounted on the wall behind the desk, as well as a rack of what might have been Civil War-era rifles. Books, magazines, junk mail, food packaging, and lots of other flotsam were piled everywhere. There was a wet bar to the left and a paned window along the back that looked out on what might have been a pool, but it was too dark to see. A leather loveseat that matched the chairs was situated under the window, one big enough for him to sleep on. The pillow and green blanket bunched in one corner led me to believe he used it for that purpose.

It was obvious he spent a lot of time in the room, not just because of the couch or the clutter, but because it smelled like him, a fragrant blend of old man sweat, garlicky food, and various varieties of booze. Tom, having hung up his trench coat, was already at the bar pouring us drinks. I drifted to one of the wingbacks, but decided not to sit because I didn't want him to get the idea I was going to stay long.

Then a silver-framed photo on the desk—the only thing on it—caught my eye. It pictured a much younger Tom Gaffin, brown-haired, baby-faced, and dressed in a tuxedo, standing next to a pert blonde in a wedding dress. They were both smiling. It was a wedding photo like so many other wedding photos, but there was something about Tom's eyes that looked haunted.

"She died," Tom said.

His voice startled me. He was standing to my left, a crystal snifter in each hand, the bourbon sloshing around inside the color of caramel.

"What's that?" I said.

"My wife. About a year after we were married."

"Oh, Jesus, I'm sorry."

He handed me one of the glasses, then gestured to the wingbacks. We both sat. I could say it was because I was more intrigued than ever about Tom Gaffin's life story, but mostly I think it was the bourbon. It smelled like heaven in a glass. I took a sip. It tasted like it too. I had to restrain myself from guzzling it.

Tom leaned into his wingback, far more worn of the two, and took a sing of his bourbon. "Yeah, here's the real kicker. It was my fault. I was drinking even worse than I drink now, if you can believe that. Plowed into the concrete underpass down on River Road—you know, the one that gets folks even today. They say I didn't even hit the brakes. Not that I remember it."

"Oh. That's ..." I fumbled for something to say, to try to connect with him or show empathy, and ended up with something pretty inane. "I … I've had my share of blackouts too."

"Well, this wasn't *that* kind of blackout, Jake, but I'll get to that in a minute. You want to know what really takes the cake? Ronnie was pregnant with our first child. I lost them both."

"Wow, I … I'm really sorry."

He nodded solemnly. I tried to think of something else to say, but I figured it would just be something else inane, so I just sat there silently. The shame he carried in his heart must have been way heavier than mine, and mine was plenty heavy. Then I thought about it a bit more, and something didn't quite make sense. It was all the stuff he'd said about Ronnie's Rules. "How long were you together before you got married?" I asked.

He took another sip of his bourbon, his gaze turning to the picture on the desk. "Not long. Six months, I think. It was love at first sight. I was a traveling salesman—kind of last of a breed, you know."

He laughed softly. I was even more confused than before, because he'd certainly implied that she'd been part of his life a lot longer than that, but maybe I was confused. Or maybe the bourbon was just going to my head.

"So," he said, lifting his glass to me, "the story of how Tom Gaffin got rich. You're not going to believe it, but I'll tell it straight anyway. It all came down to one phone call."

Then he leaned back in the chair and started to talk.

THIS HAPPENED on the last day of August, Jake. I'll never forget the exact day, partly because it was hot enough outside that I could have baked potatoes on the hood of my rusty old Buick, but mostly because it was Ronnie's birthday and that was the reason I was stopping to make a call. I'd already talked to her once that day, in the morning from the motel, where I'd promised I'd make it back to Rexton before dark. Now I needed to call to apologize. I'd had a promising new prospect on a tip from an existing client—I was selling copy machines at the time, of all things—and I needed to meet this guy first thing in the morning.

I was less than two hours from home, but I could barely afford to fill my tank as it was, and that was assuming the Buick and its balky radiator would even hold up under the strain. No way I could chance missing the sale.

I was dreading the call. Ronnie had put up with a lot from me since we'd been married, and all I did was keep dishing out disappointment. We were broke, I drank too much, and we were still living in this cottage by Barnaby Park—a tiny thing, with a big bay window almost as wide as the house. This wasn't the nice area on the west side of the park, but the southeast, where the creek sometimes flooded the neighborhood. Still, it wasn't a terrible place to live, as things go, but I wanted so much more for her. I was starting to feel like it was never going to happen.

So that was my state of mind—guilt-ridden, miserable in my sweat-stained JCPenney suit, and full of all kinds of what-ifs and might-have-beens— when I stopped at a two-pump Ma and Pa gas station in the Oregon countryside just after sunset. No, I won't say where this was, so don't ask, but I will say that it was one of the prettiest places I'd ever been, full of rolling green hills that hadn't yet started to brown under the summer sun. The sky, in those first few minutes after the sun went down, was a vibrant shade of pink that reminded me of Ronnie's favorite lipstick.

Somehow, though, all that beauty just made me feel even worse, because Ronnie wasn't with me to appreciate it. I still had a quarter tank of gas, but I figured the least I could do was fill up now so I could drive straight back after my morning meeting.

The pumps, more rust than red now, looked like they dated from the fifties. The ramshackle building, white paint flaking to gray, loomed at the back of the gravel lot. I would have driven right past under the assumption it had long since been out of business had I not spotted an old man in denim overalls in the open garage. He was as weathered and gray as one of the neighboring farm's fence posts and just as bald, leaning over a baby blue '57 Ford F-100. I knew exactly what truck it was because my father owned one when I was a child. It was his pride and joy, which was more than I could say for me.

So I pulled into the gravel lot, kicking up a cloud of dust. I sat there boiling in my Buick until the old guy trotted out to greet me. His skin was gnarled and deeply-grooved like hickory bark, he had a gap in his front teeth he could have stuck his tongue through, and his breath stank of pipe smoke.

While he filled the tank, and afraid he might want to make conversation, I got out to stretch my legs. I may have swooned to the smell of a good brandy, but I hated the scent of pipe smoke with a passion. It reminded me too much of my daddy, who used to beat me something fierce with his belt if he'd had a hard day on the dairy farm. He used to beat me on the good days, too, just not as badly.

So I was walking away from the old man, and I was avoiding looking at the truck, and I was feeling sad and lonely and wretched, when I looked through the gravel dust and the gathering haze of sunset and spotted the payphone.

It was mounted on the side of the building nearest the road, a Ma Bell special with a stainless steel front, black plastic sides, and a coin slot so scratched that the metal was more white than gray. It even had the phone book in the black plastic case dangling from a coil. There used to be thousands of payphones just like them all over the country.

I figured, why not? It was a long distance call, but

not by much, and I had an ashtray full of small change for parking meters, a necessity for a traveling salesman. I reached into the open driver side window and grabbed a handful of quarters, then sauntered over to the payphone in the fading light. I was reaching for the receiver when the old man spoke.

"Make sure you call collect," he said.

I turned and looked at him. While the pump chugged away, he was leaning against the Buick, wiping his hands on his oil-stained overalls; the denim was so dark and splotchy it looked like a Rorschach test.

"Sorry?" I said.

"I don't know why," he said, "but it's the only way it seems to work. If you put your quarters in there, it'll just eat'm for dinner."

"Collect?" I said.

"That's right, sonny. Pick up the receiver, punch zero, and an operator will come on. Just tell her you want to place a collect call. She'll connect you to who you need to talk to. Always does."

He smiled his gap-toothed smile. Even though his voice was friendly enough, there was something chilling about that smile. In the hazy light, with the gravel dust wafting over him, that gap between his teeth was black indeed. It felt like I was looking through a keyhole into a dark room. Or another person.

Then the dust passed, and I blinked, and he was again just a friendly old man in oil-stained overalls.

He nodded as if he'd given me the most sage advice in the world, then turned his attention back to the nozzle.

I picked up the receiver, faded and cracked from sun exposure, and punched zero. I'm not sure if I heard a dial tone. In my mind, there definitely was one, but I've thought about that a lot over the years and I'm not sure anymore.

"Operator," a woman said. "How may I assist you?"

Her voice was flat, as if she could barely muster the interest to even ask the question. I told her I wanted to make a collect call and gave her my home number. It rang. But the person who answered wasn't Ronnie. It was a man.

"Gaffin residence," he said.

I was so confused it took me a second to respond. It wasn't until later that I realized the operator had never asked him if he wanted to accept the collect call.

"Who is this?" I said.

"I'm sorry?" he said.

"Where's Ronnie?" I said.

"She's out right now," he said, the suspicion growing in his voice. "Can I ask who's calling?"

"It's her husband, you damn fool," I said. "Now what the hell are you doing in my house?"

When he didn't answer, I felt the first cold chill of dread, starting as a prickling along the back of my arms and spreading all the way up my spine to the back of my neck. It didn't even occur to me until later

—much later, years, in fact—that the most logical explanation for a strange man answering my phone was Ronnie having an affair. Maybe that said something about how much we loved each other, and I think it did, but I also think that some part of me knew something unusual was happening. More than unusual. *Unnatural.*

"I don't know what kind of game you're playing, mister," he said finally, "but I'm hanging up right now. Don't ever call again."

The fear in his trembling voice matched the fear in my own. In fact, it was a lot more than fear that matched, and I realized it just in time. Or not late enough, depending on how you looked at it.

"Wait," I said. "What's your name?"

"Excuse me?"

I swallowed hard. "Your name. Just tell me your name."

"Listen, pal, I don't need to tell you *anything*. Don't call again or I'm calling the cops, you got it? Now goodbye and good riddance."

"You're Tom Gaffin," I said hurriedly. "In seventh grade, you—you caught your dad in bed with Ella Contraire—Jimmy's Mom, who lived just across from the school. He cried and begged you not to say anything. You never did. After that, he didn't beat you no more."

There was a long pause. I hadn't told anybody that, not even Ronnie, but there was something about the way he'd said *goodbye and good riddance* that finally clued me in to what might be going on here, because it was a catchphrase I used all the time. A Dodge Ram hauling a horse trailer rattled past the gas station, so when he spoke again in a soft voice, I had to ask him to repeat it.

"I asked who told you about that," he said.

"Nobody," I said.

"Did you know my father?"

"Of course I did, but that's not how I know it!"

"Bullshit," he said. "I haven't told a single—"

"—soul," I finished for him. "I know. I know that too. What color was Connie Armstrong's underwear?"

"Connie?"

"Come on! We don't know how long we have here, man, and I have to know for sure. You lost your virginity with her. Senior year of high school, in her room when her parents were at the golf club. You never told anybody about her underwear, but you remember it, don't you?"

"Pink," he said. "Pink with little white hearts."

"Oh my God," I said.

"No," he said. "No, you can't possibly be—"

"What year is it?" I asked.

"What?"

"The year, the year, tell me the year!"

"1982," he said.

Forty-two years. I let the enormity of that sink in, but only for a second, because there was something happening to the connection. There was a crackle and a pop that wasn't there before, and his voice there at the end had faded in and out.

"Listen to me, Tom," I said. "We may only have a few seconds, so you listen up good. I'm going to tell you a bunch of stuff that's going to change your life, okay?"

"I still don't—"

"Shut up! I'm calling from 2024, don't you get it? Sometimes the universe throws you a bone, and this is your bone. Buy Microsoft, Tom. And Apple. Personal computers are going to be huge. And later, Amazon. Those three, just remember those three and you'll be rich. Ride all the ups and downs and keep putting more in."

"You're breaking . . . What was the … one?" he said. There were bursts of static. His voice was so faint it was like he was speaking from another planet. "I heard Microsoft and Apple, but I didn't—" It was lost in a crackle of noise.

"Tom?" I said.

There was another burst of static.

"Tom?" I said again.

"How's Ronnie?" he said finally.

"What?"

"Is she … and . . . the baby?"

"Baby? What baby?

". . . can't . . . you. The connection . . . breaking . . ."

"Microsoft, Apple, Amazon! Just remember those three things, Tom!"

"*. . . crash . . .*"

That was the last word he said. *Crash.* I didn't think anything of it at the time. I thought he might have been talking about a market crash, of all things, because of the stock tips I'd just given him, but later that word would haunt me. It would haunt me because by the time I got back to the Buick I wouldn't be sure he'd said the word at all. In fact, I was pretty sure *I* had said it, strange as that was.

I said his name a few more times, but there was no answer. There was no static either, just silence. I hit the zero again, but no operator came on. I hit it a few more times and got the same result. I put a quarter in, but the old man was right, the phone just ate it. It ate the rest of the quarters jingling in my pocket too.

Short of breath, feeling like the earth was tilting beneath me, I turned to talk to the old man, but he was gone. I leaned over so I could see the garage, but he wasn't bent over the F-100 either. On my way back to the Buick, my head started to pound. By the time I got in the car, it wasn't the Buick anymore, but the Cadillac DeVille. It didn't feel wrong either. It felt like mine.

The sky was blood red. Pulling out of the station, I glanced once more at the open garage. The truck was gone, but as I turned onto the road I caught a glimpse of a gap-toothed smile in the shadowy recesses of the garage. I hit the gas and roared out of there as fast as I could, intent on driving straight to the wife waiting for me at home, client be damned.

It wasn't until I was a mile down the road, passing through an old covered bridge, that I realized there was no wife waiting for me at home.

I didn't have a wife at all.

"SHE DIED FORTY YEARS AGO," Tom said, leaning back in his leather wingback. He tilted his glass back and forth, what little bourbon remained sloshing about at the bottom. "The worst day of my life, Jake. She was six months pregnant when I plowed into that embankment. She—she didn't like to drive. I'd just picked her up from another gal's baby shower. Can you believe that? Jesus. The little boy grew up to become a doctor too. I ran into his mother at Walmart the other day."

He stared at his bourbon for a moment, then gulped down the rest of it. While he'd been speaking, the deluge outside had become a drizzle, just a light tapping on the window. My clothes were completely dry.

"Wait a second," I said. "When did this all happen? This strange phone call?"

He hesitated. "It never did."

"Huh?"

"I mean, I *remember* making that call, but it's like I dreamed it, you see? It's like my real life and my dream life are all mixed up together. I can't tell what's real and what never happened but for anyone but me.

But if that call happened, the best I can figure is it happened about two years ago."

"But you made it sound like it happened decades ago."

"Nope. If it happened at all, it happened two years ago."

"I don't understand."

He laughed ruefully. *"You* don't understand? I've been living with this for two years—or forty-two, depending on which memory I chose to focus on—and I still don't understand it."

"But you *did* make that call?"

"I remember doing it. I remember *receiving* it too. My other life is getting more foggy by the day, Jake, but I'm not lying. You see, Ronnie and I, in that other life, we were happy, real happy, but we were dead broke for so long that we didn't feel it was right to try to bring a child into the world until our situation improved, but our situation never did. I'm a shit salesman and always was. Stupid in my choices too. I mean, who's trying to sell copy machines in this day and age? Then by the time we said to hell with it, let's have kids anyway, it was too late. She couldn't get pregnant."

He rose and walked to his desk, putting down the empty snifter and picking up the framed wedding photo, which he gazed at for a long time. I didn't hear the rain anymore.

I didn't know what to make of Tom's story. Talking to your past self? *Really?* Not only was it impossible to believe, but it didn't even make sense, full of all kinds of paradoxes and contradictions, the usual problems for any tale involving time travel. I'd figured out pretty quickly that a career in the sciences wasn't for me, when I barely scraped by with a C in Physics, and that was all the way back in high school, but even a English major could see that traveling to the past, or even communicating with your past self, just couldn't happen because that self that traveled back would change the past so that the one who traveled would never be, at least not the same.

I figured he was just messing with me. Was his wife even gone? Some of the things he'd said made it sound like they'd been married a lot longer than a few years, so maybe they'd divorced. Maybe he actually believed this nonsense. Maybe this was his way of coping, creating a fantastical tale to explain what was otherwise a familiar story of a broken marriage caused by all the usual suspects—booze, sleeping around, or worst of all, the slow fade from love to apathy to mutual contempt.

"The stock tips were good, though," Tom said finally, his back to me. "They were *damn* good, that was for sure. It really *is* how I got rich, Jake. Not that I enjoyed a minute of it other than that first year, when I could see that the Apple and Microsoft stock went absolutely bonkers, and Ronnie and I decided to have children. She got pregnant straight off. The night she died, I was actually planning on painting …

painting the nursery." He shook his head and put down the photo.

"Who do you think the old man was?" I asked.

"I don't know," he said. "Some kind of demon. Maybe the devil himself."

"Come on."

He turned to face me, one hand on the desk, wobbly on his feet. "Maybe he wasn't there at all? Maybe he was only in my mind? All I can say is, after coming home to this big, sad mansion and realizing what a shit life I'd actually lived despite the money, I went back. The pumps were rusted out even worse than before, but the phone was there. I went back, Jake. I wanted to undo it all. I would give all my fortune and my right arm to put things back the way they were. It didn't work, though. I hit zero over and over but got nothing."

"And the old man?"

"Nowhere to be found. I even asked the farmer next door, and I thought he was going to have his pit bulls chase me off his land. He said that station hadn't been used since the fifties."

He looked at his shoes. There was something about the way his face sagged, the jowls drooping, the wrinkles growing deeper, that made him seem so much older than even a few minutes ago. It wasn't just his body. He might have been dressed to the nines, but the brown slacks were wrinkled and spotted, the blue cardigan was stretched and fraying, and even his Italian shoes, as expensive and polished as they were, barely clung to his ankles, they were so loose.

"I don't know if the forty-two years was a given," he said. "I've thought a lot about this. The old man told me the operator would make sure I got to talk to who I needed to talk to. So maybe that me, that me from 1982, was the one who needed to hear from me." He shrugged. "All I can say is, the memory of that other life gets foggier by the day. I miss her so much, Jake. The memories of those extra forty years I had with her are all I got, the only thing that's kept me going, and when those are gone …"

He trailed off, his eyes taking on the rummy, unfocused gaze of a man who'd had too much to drink. Or just too much. At some point, the rain had started back up again, just a steady, soft plinking on the window with none of the earlier howling fury to go along with it, more the norm for the area. Rexton Rain, they called it. The winters were long and gray and the drizzle never stopped.

"So where was this phone, anyway?" I asked.

That seemed to shake him from his stupor. He smiled wryly. "Oh no, I won't do that to you. No way in hell—which is exactly where I'd be sending you."

"I was just curious, is all."

"Sure you were. Now let me get you that hundred."

"Oh it's not really …"

But he was already rifling inside his desk until he came up with a crisp green bill with Grant's face on it. Before I could refuse, the money was in my hand and we were standing at the French doors. He opened his mouth to speak, and I expected something profound, something to put a button on his crazy tale, but then the grandfather clock in the entryway began to chime.

"Time for my bath," he said.

"What?"

"Nine o'clock on the nose. Ronnie's Rules. The bath always helps with my insomnia, you see."

"Ah."

He clapped me on the shoulder. "Sometimes the universe throws you a bone, Jake," he said.

"Uh huh. I'm not really sure I know what that means."

"It means that even when things seem *really* bleak —you know, when you've messed up your life so much you're sure there's no finding your way out of it—sometimes the universe will do something good for you anyway. Though you might not know it at the time. I'm hoping you understand what I'm saying, Jake."

"What, you're saying this is the universe's way of saying I shouldn't take stock tips over the phone?"

His face darkened. I felt bad about it later. I felt wretched, in fact. Even though I didn't believe his story, he certainly did, and joking about another man's suffering, especially to his face, especially when he's just unburdened himself to you, is one of the cruelest things you can do to another person. It's the deepest kind of cut from the sharpest kind of blade.

"I'm saying I'm a living example that money can't give you what matters," he said. "I'm saying you should remember this when life tempts you to think otherwise. I'm saying whatever life throws your way, it's got lessons to teach you. Just own it. Own all of it, the good and the bad. It makes you who you are. It might even make you somebody worth loving."

I was speechless at that, but before I could summon the words to respond, he patted me on the shoulder one last time.

"Good luck, Jake," he said. "I'll—I'll let you see yourself out. Thanks again for the ride."

Then he turned abruptly. It was the kind of thing a man his age—hell, a man *my* age—will do when he doesn't want you to see him cry. I did what I was taught a man should do in response. I pretended it didn't happen.

When I headed for the front door, he was standing in front of the Civil War rifles mounted on the wall. It didn't mean anything to me in the moment, but it should have. Christ, I was an English major. I'd read plenty of Chekhov.

I heard the shotgun when I was getting into the Corvette.

IT WASN'T until late summer, long after Tom's funeral, that I really started thinking about his story again—or more specifically, about the phone. Mostly it came from desperation. It was hard to believe, because I'd thought waiting tables at Denny's would be the low point of my life, but I'd spiraled much farther down the drain by that point. The drinking got worse. Megs canned me. She said it was for calling in sick too many times, but I think it was also for all the days I came in without remembering to pop a few Altoids in my mouth first.

It wasn't just the Altoids I forgot. I forgot to pick up Ella from school—not just once, but three times, and Julia went back to the judge to ask for full custody. By May I was scraping by on measly unemployment checks and mowing lawns for some former clients, plus drinking even heavier because of the humiliation of it all. By August I was living out of my Corvette because I had to choose between making rent or the child support payments.

So I started thinking about Tom Gaffin's story again, first idly, just wondering what I would say to my former self that would change the trajectory of my life, and then a lot more seriously, as I found myself staring at a light that wasn't the end of a tunnel but the top of the drain. I was holding onto the lip by my fingernails. Could the phone *actually* be real? At the funeral, I'd confirmed that the sad tale of his young pregnant wife dying in a car accident was true, as was his early life as a mediocre traveling salesman. I got it all from Perry Henshaw, a former colleague who couldn't recall any of Tom's routes, other than to say he remembered Tom worked the Eugene area quite a bit.

The only other people at the funeral were two distant cousins, each of whom had refused to talk to me. I think they were both trying to make claims to the estate and regarded me with suspicion.

It was Ella, of all people, who finally supplied the missing piece.

"Knock knock, Daddy," she said.

It was Saturday. We were in the Corvette, waiting for the stoplight in the McDonald's parking lot on Commercial. It smelled like the greasy French Fries in Ella's Happy Meal box. The sun glowed like a branding iron on the yellow hood. We'd only been in the car a few minutes and already sweat beaded on my forehead. The air conditioner was starting to go, and the lukewarm air blowing out of the vents struggled to keep the blazing heat at bay.

"Who's there?" I said, idly scratching the rough stubble on my chin.

"Cottage," she said.

"Cottage who?"

"Cottage Cheese!" she cried, clapping her hands together in unrestrained glee.

I smiled at her, this bouncy, blonde bundle of joy squirming in her car seat. She may not have quite gotten the knack for a good knock-knock joke, but she made up for it with pure enthusiasm. Oh, and volume too. She was not a quiet kid.

I wondered how much longer she'd take joy from such simple pleasures. I also wondered how much longer she'd look at me as one of the heroes of her life despite all evidence to the contrary. In three weeks she'd be starting second grade. Would I even get to pick her up from school by that point?

Not if Julia had her way. When I picked Ella up a half hour ago, from that pretty striver's house in Oak Heights that once was mine, my ex-wife appraised the sad sack of a man standing on her porch, with his two-day beard, his bloodshot eyes, and his breath reeking of Altoids *and* Listerine, and warned me that if I ever, *ever* showed up drunk to pick up Ella, I could forget about having visitation rights, much less any sort of shared custody.

This Saturday may have been the last unsupervised day I'd have with my daughter for the foreseeable future, and I wanted to make the most of it. When Ella made her joke, I'd been tapping on the hot leather steering wheel and debating whether to take her to a movie, or to The Enchanted Grove, the little amusement park south of town. I would prefer the movie, and its blessed air conditioning, but I knew Ella would choose the amusement park regardless of the weather.

It was her joke that got me thinking about Tom's story again. There'd been a clue buried within it I'd completely forgotten.

"Cottage Grove," I mumbled.

"No, Daddy, cottage *cheese.*"

"What? Oh, right. Yes, that's a good one, dear. No, Cottage Grove is a city south of Eugene. I've never been there, but I just remembered that they bill themselves as the covered bridge capital of Oregon."

Ella, forehead furrowing, dipped into her Happy Meal for another French Fry. "Why do bridges need covers?"

"Well, they're made of wood, and it helps protect them. Some are very old. How would you like to go see some of them?"

"Can we get ice cream?"

"Sure, kiddo, but only after we see the bridges. It's a bit of a drive, so you have to be good the whole way. Can you be good?"

She clapped her hands and promised to be *very* good. Oh, to be seven years old again, and so easily pleased. I couldn't remember anything making me so happy in years, but already my heart was pounding at the possibility of a different kind of life.

The light changed and I turned south on the boiling blacktop, heading for the interstate. It was a two-hour drive, nothing for me, but an eternity for a kid her first-grade teacher suggested might be ADHD. I figured Ella's hyperactivity was more due to the trauma from the divorce, which was on me.

There was a lot one phone call could fix. *A lot.*

She barely made it twenty minutes before she started to complain. When she spotted the sign for

The Enchanted Grove looming over the freeway—I'd stupidly forgotten to distract her—she insisted we stop. When I told her no, she began to cry. I gave her my phone. The dozen games on there kept her busy until we passed Albany, but then she tossed the phone into the foot well and announced she wanted to go home.

I reminded her about the ice cream. That bought me another ten minutes. Then she said she needed to use the bathroom. We stopped at a rest area at the Highway 20 junction to Corvallis, where I filled my gas-guzzling tank and she managed enough of a tinkle to be respectable, and I bought her a bag of M&Ms to prevent another meltdown. Mercifully, she fell asleep as we roared past Eugene, and didn't wake until I was nearing the exit for Cottage Grove.

"It's hot in here, daddy," she said.

"Is it?"

I smiled at her, but Ella was all out of smiles. I tried to hand her a bottled water, but she crossed her arms and glared. She was giving me the same squinty, puckered-lips look that Julia gave me when she was pissed. For Ella to comment on the heat meant it had to be bad indeed, but even though my T-shirt and jeans stuck to me like snakeskin, I'd been so focused on what I wanted to say to my former self that I hadn't really noticed.

After I convinced past-Jake with a childhood memory I'd never shared with anyone, most of what I'd say came down to this: *You're an alcoholic, Jake. Seek help before you ruin your life the way I did. Before it's too late to do anything about it. Oh, and put a couple thousand into Amazon when it has its IPO and let it ride for a decade.*

"Can we have ice cream now?" Ella asked.

"Soon, kiddo. Real soon."

She started to cry again, so I amended our deal and we swung through the drive-thru at the Dairy Queen as soon as we entered town. On a blazing hot Saturday, it was no surprise that there were six cars in line ahead of us, but that was all right. It gave me a few minutes, as a freight train kicked up a cloud of dust right next to us, to do some Googling with my smartphone. Before we'd even made it to the window, I'd not only downloaded a very nice map to all the covered bridges in the area courtesy of the Cottage Grove Chamber of Commerce, I'd selected three I thought would be good candidates.

Remote. Near farmland. Even using Google Earth, I couldn't find any obvious old filling stations, but there were so many groves of oak, maple, and fir trees that I figured it was just invisible from space.

I *hoped* the station was just invisible from space. That was how much my attitude had changed from when I'd first heard Tom's fantastical tale. I'd gone from blatant dismissiveness, to vaguely entertaining the possibility that maybe, just maybe, it might be real, to actually counting on that mystical phone call to set things right.

My hopes were soon dashed. An hour later, long

after Ella had finished her Oreo blizzard, I'd checked out the three covered bridges I'd plugged into my phone's GPS, plus the other three proudly listed on the map, but there was nothing remotely like the filling station Tom had described. No payphone mounted on the side of a dilapidated building. No old man peering out of an open-air garage. The scenery was certainly lush, with lots of rolling green hills and plenty of picturesque red barns, but I was in no mood to enjoy it.

I drove farther afield, checking out a few other covered bridges in Lane County, and had no luck with them either. I returned to Cottage Grove and hit all six of their bridges again. We even got out and explored a few, the old boards creaking under our feet. No dice. By this time, I'd ignored both the text message and the phone call from Julia asking where I was.

If I didn't call her by seven o'clock, more than an hour after I was supposed to drop off Ella at her house, she'd probably call the police on me.

Scratch that. She'd *definitely* call the police on me. A text to say I was running late would no longer suffice. I'd have to call her, and for some reason I was absolutely convinced that when I did, whatever chance I had that Tom's magical phone was real, would vanish as soon as the banal reality of Julia's inevitable diatribe hit my ears.

"I want to go home," Ella said.

"Just a little longer, dear."

"This isn't fun, Daddy."

"Oh, come on. It isn't so bad. How about we sing a song?"

"No."

"Row, row, row your boat? You like that one."

"I hate that song!"

"Okay, okay. We could try a different—"

"No! No singing!"

"Ella—"

It was too late. She was working herself into an outright tantrum, crying, banging on her armrests, the whole deal, and that would have been the end of our sad little adventure if I hadn't swung around one last bend, far out in the countryside west of Cottage Grove, and spotted a ramshackle white building, two rust red gas pumps, and an open-aired garage with the baby blue hood of a '57 Ford F-100 just visible in the shadowy interior.

"Oh my God," I said.

Usually even a superhuman parental effort wasn't enough to derail Ella from one of her fits once she'd started, but there must have been something in my voice that startled her, because all the screaming and banging abruptly stopped.

"Daddy?" she said.

"This is it, Ella. This is it."

"But I don't see a bridge!"

"What? Oh, right. The bridge—the bridge I'm looking for comes later. First I want to stop here. I … I need gas again."

I found myself short of breath, because I'd spotted the payphone on the side of the building—stainless steel front, black plastic sides, and a phone book dangling from a metal coil. I was sure I'd passed this same spot three times already, and yet none of it was here before. With the sun low in the west, the shadow of the garage fell over the pumps and most of the gravel lot.

We skidded to a halt and I popped open my door before the dust had even settled. The old man wasn't there.

"Can I get out, Daddy?"

"No, honey. You stay here."

"But I'm hot, Daddy."

"I'll roll down the windows, okay? It'll just be for a minute."

"I don't feel good, Daddy."

"I won't be long. Please. This is very important."

My hands shaking, I retrieved the McDonald's bag I'd tossed behind my seat and set it on her tiny lap. I told her that if she felt like she was going to throw up, to do it in the bag. She started to tear up, but I didn't know how long I had, and I couldn't waste precious seconds placating her.

By the time I had the black plastic receiver in my hand, Ella was crying again. It was so quiet—a few crickets, the distant rumble of a freight train—that I had no trouble hearing her across the gravel parking lot. I would have had no trouble hearing a dial tone, either, if there'd been one.

I hit zero anyway. Nothing happened. I punched it a few more times, each time more violently, but still nothing. I closed my eyes and pressed the receiver against my sweaty forehead, the plastic warm from baking in the sun. The air smelled of burnt oil, dry grass, and more faintly, the manure that must have been used to fertilize the nearby farm. There were no other cars. I heard the cawing of a crow, then, rising above the warm breeze rustling the live oaks on the other side of the road, the trickle of a distant brook. It was so quiet I could hear the beating of my own heart.

Too quiet. I looked in Ella's direction and was alarmed to see an old man—lanky in his denim over-alls, his head as bald as the hood of my Corvette— leaning down to the passenger window. The sun, grazing the top of the building, left the windshield half in shadow and half in light, and I couldn't make out Ella inside.

"Hey!" I shouted at him.

The old man leaned back, peering at me with a bemused, tight-lipped smile. It was actually his shadow, as he stood into the sunlight, that allowed me to see that Ella was still in her car seat. Not only that, but she was smiling, which should have made me feel better, but actually unnerved me even more.

"Your daughter's cute as a button, sonny," the old man said. "Funny as heck too. I always wish I had a daughter like that."

There was something vaguely menacing about his

tone, and I realized how stupid I'd been, how incredibly stupid. Hadn't Tom warned me that the old man might be the devil himself? And here I'd delivered my precious little girl straight into his oil-stained hands.

We stared at each other across the gravel parking lot, the air hazy with dust, the light already losing its color.

"You want me to top her off?" the old man asked.

"What?"

He wiped his hands on his overalls. "I don't got any of the fancy premium stuff, but I think your old Corvette would choke on it, to be honest."

"Oh. Um, no. No, that's okay. I just ..."

"Stopped to make a call? That's fine. Just make sure you call collect, sonny. Don't reckon I know why, but it's the only way it works. Hit zero and a nice lady will come on. She'll put it through."

He smiled again, and this time it wasn't a tight-lipped smile but one that revealed the gap in his teeth. Tom had been right about how big and dark that space between his yellowed front teeth was, like a glimpse at something hiding inside the old man, something just using his skin to get around in the world.

I debated about putting down the receiver and taking off in the Corvette right then, phone call be damned, but I'd come too far, and I needed the salvation that call would bring me too much, to scurry away now.

I punched zero. This time, an operator came on, a

woman with a flat voice. I told her I wanted to make a collect call and gave her the number. It started to ring, and it was only at this point that the old man sauntered toward the garage. I watched him go with growing relief. I hadn't seen it before now, but a red bandana dangled from his back pocket.

Only it wasn't red. It was white, or at least it used to be. It was heavily stained with paint, ketchup, or …

"Hello?"

A man's voice, slurred. Christ, he was drunk. *I* was drunk. But was it really me? I adjusted the receiver; the plastic felt like it was burning my ear.

"Jake Conroy?" I said.

"Yeah?"

"How much have you had to drink?"

"What?"

The answer to my question was *a lot,* given not only his slurred voice but the long pauses. "Forget it. What year is it?"

"What *year?* Who—who is this?"

"Just tell me the damn year!"

"Listen, man, I'm—I'm hanging up. You got the … number, so just—"

"Shut up, you idiot," I said, my panic rising because I heard the first crackle of static. It didn't really matter what year it was, because I'd only had that number for the three years I'd lived at Chase Village in Eugene, before law school, before Julia, but when my drinking first started getting bad. I'd hoped I'd get the me in year one, when I only imbibed at the occasional frat party, and not the me in year three, when I spent more time blackout drunk than sober, but here we were. What the hell was I doing, wasting precious time? It was the old man. He'd gotten me so rattled I'd forgotten what I'd rehearsed.

Before my past self could say anything else, I launched into the details of my childhood that nobody else knew, three of them in a row, rapid fire, to leave no doubt. When I was done, he was quiet for a few seconds, then when he spoke he sounded a lot less drunk and a lot more afraid.

"Who are you?"

"I'm *you,* stupid. Haven't you figured that out? I'm calling from the future."

"No … no way. Come on."

This time the pause wasn't static; it was his booze-soaked brain trying to maintain a coherent thought. "Jesus," I said, "how drunk *are* you?"

"What does that have—?"

"Real drunk, by the sounds of it. I don't trust you to remember this. You got some paper? You need to write this down. You won't believe it unless you write it down. I'm going to change your life."

"I—I don't—"

"Top drawer under the microwave. Come on!"

I heard a drawer opening, then him rifling inside. The static got worse. I could picture the second floor apartment in the beige multiplex on the other side of the Willamette River. I could picture the green laminate countertop, the refrigerator door covered with poems my girlfriend at the time—Stacy, oh Stacy with the long lovely legs—wrote for me using word magnets, and the Far Side wall calendar hanging next to the metal sink.

I saw all this as clearly as I saw the scratched coin slot in front of me. I also saw what *wasn't* visible—the crushed beer cans under the bed, the bottle of vodka under the sink hidden behind the drain pipe—and I could feel it, how close I was to changing all of that, to getting me on the road to a better life, and it was then that my head started to pound. It was the mother of all headaches, like my swelling brain was trying to push my eyeballs out of their sockets.

I looked over at the Corvette. The sky behind the car was as red as the old man's bandana. The glare on the windshield was gone, and I could see Ella just fine now. She was looking at me.

Her hair, so yellow, so vibrant, made me think of the gold tinsel the two of us hung on the pathetic fir tree I'd bought on Christmas Eve last year, just before the lot closed up. Would we ever get to do that again? Maybe it was the hazy air, but I could actually see the blue of her eyes even across the gravel parking lot, the same blue as my own, and I thought of the sapphire earrings I gave Julia on our first Valentine's Day, a few months after we started dating in law school. It was the same night she told me she wanted children someday, so if I didn't, then I needed to break up with her now. I told her I wanted children too. I told her I'd always wanted to be a dad, and a good one, maybe not as good as my dad, because how could I compare, how could *any* man compare, but I'd do my best. I'd always do my best.

In a way, it was like she'd proposed and I'd said yes, because a year later we were married.

It was true, all of this. And thinking about it now, with the hot plastic against my ear and the sound of rustling paper on the other end of the line, I thought about how bad the drinking got after Dad died, always bad but not *this* bad. And I thought about my promise to Julia. And I thought most of all about the little girl buckled into the car seat that was buckled into the passenger seat—that stupid car, the last damn thing I owned of any value, and I'd always thought it was so precious, my pride and joy, but that wasn't true.

It was Ella. It was always Ella. And if I helped the guy on the phone change his life, there was a chance Ella would never be.

"Hello?" my younger self said. "Are … there?"

The wind stirred the dust around the Corvette, swirled it into a tiny cyclone that soon dispersed. For such a warm evening, the wind was cold and bitter. I shivered. I looked over at the open garage, and there was the old man leaning against the front of his old truck, looking right back at me. He smiled his gap-toothed smile, and it was like that dark space in his mouth was even darker, so cold and so dark.

"What is it?" my younger self, his voice crackling with static. "What is it you … to tell me?"

The pounding in my head had spread to my ears, so I could barely hear him. I could barely hear the wind. I thought of what I'd rehearsed, the little speech that would change my life.

Then I told him something I hadn't rehearsed at all.

It was a long drive home, especially with my ears ringing from the hell Julia gave me when I called to tell her I was going to be late. She demanded to know where I was, and I couldn't very well lie, because I knew Ella wouldn't be able to keep it secret even if I'd asked her. Which I didn't. And wouldn't. Not now, not ever. I'd never ask Ella to lie for me. I didn't know if Julia would ever take me back, or even if I wanted that now, but damned if I wasn't going to be the father Ella deserved.

She was seven years old. She loved knock-knock jokes. She was the best thing that had ever happened to me.

Leaving the station, the old man hadn't said anything, but he did give me a little wave as I roared out of the parking lot. I saw him in my rearview mirror, still leaning against the old Ford. He wasn't smiling. I didn't know if that was good or bad, but I was never going back to find out. It wasn't until we'd reached the interstate that I'd even summoned the courage to ask Ella what the old man had said to her. She asked me what old man I was talking about.

The headache was gone before I'd even passed Eugene. Ella slept most of the way. She was still sleeping when I took the first Rexton exit, not the fastest way back to Julia's place—I might as well get used to calling it that—but I had one more stop to make. A little house by Barnaby Park.

I knew exactly where to go. I'd already driven past once a few months back, on a pleasant Sunday afternoon in June, just to satisfy my curiosity. It was still a tiny ranch house with a big bay window, though the yellow paint looked fresh, there was a deck on the backside in the process of being built, and a young Hispanic couple were the ones doing the building. A boy that looked like a cross between them climbed the apple tree in the yard.

This time, when I passed the house, it was just before ten o'clock. It was a clear night; the stars were even visible over the top of the roof, a rare thing in perpetually overcast Rexton. It was so clear that I could easily see into the lighted living room, through the big bay window that was indeed as wide as the tiny house. They hadn't yet closed the curtains.

Inside, an old man sat on a couch watching television. He was alone. I could only see the back of his head. As I slowed the Corvette to a crawl, trying to make out as much as I could, my rumbling engine must have caught his attention, because he turned and peered out the window.

It was Tom Gaffin.

I slowed the car even more, feeling relieved that my young, drunk-out-of-his-mind self had not only written down the address I'd given him correctly, but mailed the letter. The Corvette drifted to a stop, idling in front of that little cottage as Tom leaned out even farther to stare at me with curiosity. He looked younger and healthier than when I'd joined him at his mansion, and I hoped the reason he looked healthier, so much healthier, was because my past self had written down the rest I'd wanted in the letter too: *Money can't give you what matters. Remember this when you're tempted to think otherwise.*

I'd been afraid to say more, for fear of changing things too much, but I felt I owed Tom that much at least. Sometimes the universe throws you a bone, and he'd thrown me a big one. I didn't know if I could turn my life around, but I was going to give it my all, with a call to the AA hotline as soon as I got home. Idling there in the middle of the road, with the two of us staring at each other across time and space, I was glad he hadn't killed himself, but I'd hoped for so much more. I wanted him to have the happiness he deserved.

Then an old woman stepped into view.

She looked a lot like the woman in the wedding photo I'd seen on Tom's desk in that mansion he would never own. Silver hair instead of blonde, of course. She was carrying a bowl of popcorn, which she handed to her husband. He said something to her and nodded toward the window. She laughed.

She was still laughing when she closed the curtains.

———

So I'm sitting here typing this in my crappy apartment, on a ten-year-old laptop I only still own because the pawnshop wouldn't give me money for it, and I'm typing it fast because I know that I'm probably going to forget all this soon enough. It's already getting all mixed up in my head. Did I really go to Tom Gaffin's mansion? Tomorrow, when I go back to Denny's to beg Megs to give me one more chance, I doubt I'll remember Tom ever coming there. I'll probably tell myself it was the product of a blackout drunk dream.

But I *did* call AA when I got home. And I *am* going to do better. I thought about changing the city, but I decided to leave it true. Go ahead. Go there, if you're brave enough. Make your call. Maybe you're willing to take that chance. No matter what happens, though, don't blame me. It's all on you. Own it, whatever happens.

Just make sure you call collect.

MEETING ON A PARK BENCH

THE OLD MAN took a seat on the park bench at exactly noon. Right on time. He wore tan khakis, a salmon-colored golf shirt, and a black baseball cap with a silver patch Todd couldn't quite make out, even with his binoculars. A college mascot, maybe? The logo looked like a bird or a lizard. Not that it mattered much. Todd never cared about the little details. As he often joked to the other guys, he just had to deliver the chocolate. He didn't need to know where the chocolate came from or what happened to it after he left.

The old man was alone and he carried a Neiman Marcus leather satchel. Barnaby Park in Rexton, Oregon. The first Saturday in July. That's all that mattered. The important stuff.

As far as meeting places went, it wasn't bad—a new wooden bench on a fresh concrete pad, with a sweeping view of the grassy field below—but Todd was baffled why the guy had chosen a spot with no shade. Even in Todd's air-conditioned rental car, he felt the oppressive sun bearing down on him. He'd been in Portland for a delivery almost exactly a year ago, only forty miles north, and the weather had been nothing like this. He hated wearing his leather jacket, but the jacket hid his side holster, and he didn't like going anywhere without his piece.

When Todd was satisfied that the old man was truly alone, he got out and took the long way under the canopy of oaks that provided at least a little relief from the heat, swinging by the pioneer statue. He pretended to answer his cell phone and chatted with an imaginary brother about how blistering hot the weather was.

Blistering wasn't even a strong enough word. When Todd stepped out of the dappled shade onto the concrete pad, it felt like he was stepping onto the surface of the sun. Under his leather jacket, his shirt was already sticking to his back.

"Okay, okay, see you soon, pal," Todd said, and pretended to click off. He smiled at the old man, just two strangers in a park. "Hey, you mind if I sit? Got a few minutes to kill."

Kill. It wasn't a good word choice given the nature of their meeting, but then nobody was around to hear it but the two of them. The old man tilted his head back, squinting at him. Without the hat brim to shade his face, the guy was looking straight into the sun. He didn't look like he got much sun, that was for sure. With his deep jowls, he looked a little like Walter Matthau. Or maybe the corpse of Walter Matthau.

"Sure, sure, no problem," the old man said. He picked up his satchel, which had been sitting on the bench next to him, and placed it on his lap. "I'm not saving this seat for anyone special."

There it was. The code words. *I'm not saving this seat for anyone special.* The Company told the delivery guys one item of clothing to look for—in this case a Neiman Marcus satchel—and then a sentence the client would have to say to verify they'd paid. Now Todd just needed a name and address.

He sat. The bench, a rich, honey oak, still smelled of oil, but it wasn't tacky. The bronze dedication plate had been polished to within an inch of its life. Now for the part Todd hated. In theory, the client *could* just give him the info straight off, but in practice they almost never did. They usually needed some bullshit small talk.

"Hot," Todd said.

"Sure is," the old man said.

"Nice bench, though."

"It is, it is. I ..."

The old guy trailed off, his voice hoarse. Todd tensed. Every now and then a client had second thoughts, worrying whether they were the kind of person who could order chocolate to be delivered. Which was fine. The money was nonrefundable. The problem was when clients had a full-on meltdown.

When that happened, they sometimes got loud and talkative about things that couldn't be said.

It almost never happened, though. All clients knew the price they'd pay for any funny business. The client purchased the chocolate through an anonymous exchange using crypto. An employee showed up to get a name and address in person. If something happened to the delivery boy, the Company would not only deliver chocolate to the client, but also to the wife, the kids, the parents, and anyone else the client cared about. That was a lot of chocolate. Almost no client wanted to pay that kind of price, which was why the Company was so successful.

Was the old guy going to say the name or not? It was too damn hot to wait around any longer. "Well," Todd said, "guess I'll shove off. Got to meet my brother. Have a nice day now."

"Wait," the old guy said. "I'm … I'm waiting for someone too."

"Ah."

"Steve Nichols. He … he should show up any minute."

Todd nodded. They were back in business. "Your friend live around here?" he asked.

The old guy clutched his satchel as if afraid Todd was going to steal it. Then, exhaling a long, rattling breath, he stood. He took a few unsteady steps, then turned and blurted out the address.

Bingo. Todd still got paid even if a client backed

out, but he preferred to do the delivery. It wasn't so much about earning it. He just enjoyed the work. The old man wiped tears from his face, sniffling. Jesus. This could still go bad. The way the old man hunched over in the sun, pale and kind of warped, even his golf shirt and khakis faded and old, he made Todd think of a badly melted candle, one that didn't have much wick left.

"Don't you need to get on with things?" Todd asked.

"Yes," the old man said. "Yes, that's … that's it exactly. I need to get on with things. But I want to talk to you about something first."

With an exasperated sigh, Todd unzipped his jacket, knowing this would give the old guy a glimpse of the holster. "Maybe you should get going instead."

"Look under the bench," the old man said.

"Excuse me?"

"Don't get up. Just look."

"You know what happens if you mess with an order, right?"

"Look. *Now.*"

The old guy's eyes were still bleary, but his tone was forceful. Todd didn't like it, but he looked under the bench. He only meant to take a quick glance, but what he saw sent a blast of ice water through his veins.

A wooden box, half the size of a shoebox, was attached to the slats, either with glue or screws. The bottom of the box was open, revealing two metal cylinders, red and black wires, and some sort of electronic device. The box was roughly the same yellowish color as the wood, so it would have been tough for Todd to see except from below.

"It's pressure-sensitive," the old man said. "It needs … It needs at least a hundred pounds of pressure or it … well, to use your company's terminology, makes its delivery. There's no outrunning it, trust me. Oh, and it's sensitive to noise too. Just loud noises. Like … gunshots."

"Is this some kind of prank?"

"I wouldn't test that premise if I were you."

"If I get up, you'll go with me."

"I know."

"You know and you don't care?"

"Oh, I care. Believe me, I care a lot. Just not about my life anymore."

Todd's fear was already giving way to rage. "You better deactivate it right now, man. You do know what will happen if you don't, right? "

"If you'd really noticed what I'm wearing, you might not have sat down in the first place."

"What?"

The old man pointed at his cap. "I'm sure it was hard to make out from a distance, but you should have been able to tell what it was when you walked up."

Todd squinted at it. The logo he'd thought might have been a frog or a bird was actually something more elaborate: a bomb, the kind dropped from a warplane, set against a shield, with lightning bolts coming out of either side and a garland along the bottom.

"Guys in the service call it the crab," the old man said, "because the patch does kind of look like one. But it can only be earned by completing the Naval School of Explosive Ordnance Disposal. That was my job in 'Nam, you see—EOD Specialist. Basically, we diffused bombs. I was very good. And it almost ruined me. PTSD. Addicted to pain killers. It was my wife who saved me. If it wasn't for her, I would have died a long time ago."

Todd swallowed. "What do you want? Money? I have a thousand in my wallet. I can get you more."

The old man ignored this. "Few people would recognize the patch, of course, but a logo of a bomb should have raised alarm bells. And didn't you wonder why I was sitting here in the hot sun when I could have picked so many other places?"

"You *really* don't want to do this, man. You know what the Company will do."

"Oh, they're not going to do anything, Todd."

Now *that* did raise alarm bells. "How did you know my name?"

"You're sloppy, Todd. You don't notice things. It makes you bad at your job. So when I made the Company a special offer, a kind of two-for-one deal, they were quick to take it."

So they'd sold him out, the bastards. Todd's whole body was so greased with sweat that he felt as if he'd just jumped in a sauna, but it wasn't just the heat getting to him. He was staring down his own death. But he had one more play. Careful with his movements, he reached into his holster and pulled out his Ruger.

"Okay, listen," Todd said, pointing his gun at the old man. "You're—you're going to disarm this thing. You're going to do it now."

The old man frowned. "I told you the device was also sensitive to loud noises, right?"

"Yeah, but you'll die first. I'll make sure of that."

"So? I was prepared to die anyway. Two for one, remember?"

At first, Todd didn't know what to make of this— and then he did. "You're Steve Nichols? The name you gave me, that's you?"

"Right."

"You actually took out a hit on yourself? For real?"

"Ah, we're not supposed to use that language, remember? But yes, that was the only way the Company would go for it. So go ahead, pull the trigger. Or you could listen instead. Because there is still a way out of this for you."

Todd glanced around. One guy nearly jogged up by the bark chips, but he wasn't looking their way, and the rhododendron bushes blocked the view from the rest of the park. Todd could have yelled for help, but what would that get him if the old man really had a suicide wish?

"Why me?" Todd asked. "What did I ever do to you?"

"We'll get to that. If you'd been paying attention, even when I said my name the first time, it should have made you wary."

"I don't know you. I swear, we've never met."

"I don't dispute it. And as I said, I'll explain in a moment. First, put down your gun—slowly, without leaving the bench—and kick it my way."

"No way."

"I have a remote, Todd. In this satchel. It can disarm the device. I'll give it to you, but first you have to give up the gun."

"Give me the satchel."

With a sigh, the old man started to turn away. "Goodbye, Todd. Shoot me if you want."

"Okay, okay! I'll do it."

The old man stopped, eyebrows raised. Bending over without taking his weight off the bench, Todd set the Ruger on the concrete. He kicked it the old man's way. The old man picked it up, opened his satchel, and dropped it inside. Todd half-expected the guy to bolt, since he didn't really have to honor his end of the deal, and that was what Todd would have done. Instead the old man pulled a black plastic device out of his satchel.

He approached just close enough to hand it to Todd. It was an old mobile phone, with a number pad and a tiny screen. As Todd peered closely, he saw that there were green-glowing digits on the screen, counting down. *53 ... 54 ...*

"What the hell!" Todd exclaimed.

"Quiet now. Remember what I said about the noise. I'll tell you how to disarm it, but first just listen."

"Man, this isn't funny! Tell me the code."

The old guy was crying again. "Do you remember the delivery you did in Portland last year? A stock broker in Forest Park?"

"Okay, sure," Todd said, feeling a creeping desperation take hold. "But what has that got to do with—"

"He ran, right? You missed the first two shots. Like I said, you're sloppy. Well, my wife happened to be hiking with a girlfriend of hers nearby, just up there visiting for the day. One of those stray bullets struck her carotid artery ... Killed her almost instantly."

"That's what this is about?"

"Yes."

"Okay, what do you want, an apology? I'm sorry, man. I'm really sorry. Now give me the code! We're—we're under thirty seconds!"

The old guy shook his head. "I had to get your gun away from you, you see. That was the one thing I was worried about—you shooting someone. Not me. Like I said, I'm dying one way or the other. But I couldn't have you shooting a random person just out of spite. Or threatening to do it."

"Please," Todd begged, staring helplessly at the screen. *20 ... 19 ...* "Please, just tell me the code."

"I'm giving you this last chance—for my wife. She was a better person than me. All you have to do is remember her name."

"What?"

"The keypad lists three letters next to each number. Enter her name using the letters associated with those numbers. It proves that she meant something to you. That you felt at least a smidge of regret. You would have read the news, followed the story, something."

"I ... I don't ..."

"I'll give you a clue. Her name is four letters, just like yours. Four letters, four digits."

"I don't remember it."

"What you mean is, you didn't know it in the first place. You don't notice anything do you, Todd?"

"Someone else might get hurt!" Todd yelled, seeing that the count had now reached fifteen. "In the park! You want that on your conscience? If someone gets close—"

"That's the other reason I have to stand here," the old man said. "To make sure that doesn't happen."

Ten ... nine ...

"Please," Todd said. "Steve. Mr. Nichols."

Eight ... seven...

"Mr. Nichols now, is it?" the old man said. "I told you that my name should have made you wary. If you looked back even once, you'd remember."

Six ... five ... four ...

Todd stared at the timer, only seconds remaining. Her name. What could it be?

Three ...

And then Todd realized the old guy was speaking literally. The name. Looking back. It all came to him, then.

Two ...

The freshly laid concrete. The brand new bench.

One ...

The plaque.

Todd whirled around, having just enough time to absorb the words etched in bronze before everything erupted in flames:

GWEN NICHOLS, BELOVED WIFE.

THE LITTLE LIBRARY THIEF

"Can you repeat that, sir?" the woman asked. "They're stealing what, exactly?"

The dispatcher had the voice of a chain smoker, low and rough, the words like gravel tumbling in Gavin's ear drums. Yet, strangely, she also sounded kind. It gave him hope. As he clutched the phone against his ears in the sweaty stillness of the house—a landline of all things, Stacey had insisted they have a landline—he felt himself desperate for a little hope. Any hope.

"Books from the library," he said.

"They're stealing library books?"

"No, books from my Little Free Library. I just call it Little Library for short. You know, the ones you have out in front of your—"

"Oh, *those*. Right."

"They're taking all of them."

"Who?"

"I don't know! That's the point!"

"Sir, you need to stay calm. I'm happy to file your report, but—"

"Who would steal children's books, for God's sake?"

"You say it was children?"

"What?"

"Who stole the books? You saw them?"

"No! I didn't see anyone."

"Oh."

"I just . . . Can't you do something? I made this for my wife."

"Made what for your wife, sir?"

"The Little Free Library!"

"Sir, please remain calm. Did your wife see who stole them?"

"What? No! She's not . . . she's not . . . I don't see how this is relevant. Can't an officer come out and, I don't know, watch it or something?"

"But, sir, didn't you just say the books were gone?"

"Huh?"

"If the books are gone, what is there for an officer to watch?"

"I keep putting more in!"

"Ah. I mean, can't someone just take a book if they want? Isn't that how it's supposed to work?"

"But not all of them at once! If they take all of them, they're stealing!"

"Please remain calm, sir. All right, then, your wife. Would it be possible to speak to her, please?"

He hung up on her. So much for hope.

THREE WEEKS EARLIER, when the cherry blossom tree in his front yard was just starting to bloom, UPS dropped the cardboard box on his doorstep. Gavin had no idea what was inside.

Four months, two weeks, ten days. That was how long it had been and *still* he was getting all kinds of packages in the mail. A green cashmere scarf from Land's End, bought during the Christmas season but arriving only last week because they'd been out of stock. A weird plastic gizmo from Wayfair that seemed like some sort of kitchen utensil. Dish soap from Amazon, part of the regular monthly order that he kept forgetting to change.

The box was huge. When Gavin opened the door to find the thing sitting on his concrete stoop, he could hear the UPS man muttering as he clambered into his idling van. It was more of a crate, really, part cardboard, part plywood, big enough that Gavin could probably squeeze inside himself, especially with how much weight he'd lost lately. Studying the box, he scratched the rough stubble on his chin. L.L LOVELY was written on the side, in pale gray letters meant to look stenciled by hand but was actually a font Gavin recognized from when he used to work as a graphic designer.

"My daughter has one of those," a woman said.

He looked up to find an old lady standing at the end of his driveway. He thought the words *old lady*, though he realized right away that she was probably younger than him. Her silver hair made her look old, but both her bright brown eyes and her wide, friendly smile radiated a youthful energy. Attractive, he thought, and then felt guilty for it. She wore a pink cardigan the same color as the cherry blossoms.

"Excuse me?" he said. The evening breeze, smelling of his neighbor's freshly-mowed grass, streamed past his bare legs. He tightened his bathrobe.

"A Little Free Library," the woman said. "My daughter bought hers from the same company. I'm so glad you're putting one up."

"Oh," Gavin said.

"I'm new here, by the way. Name's Fay. I live over on Whitley, by the park. Moved here to be close to my . . . my daughter . . ."

She trailed off, gaping at him, and he knew why. He could feel it happening even before she stopped speaking, a hot welling of grief rising up from his stomach, into his throat, his face. If he'd had time to prepare himself, if he'd had any inclination that this box was arriving, he might have been able to weather the storm, but coming like this, so unexpectedly, he had no chance.

"Oh God," Fay said, "I'm sorry. Did I say something wrong? Are you—are you okay? Is there anything I can—"

She was still speaking when he closed the door.

THE PREVIOUS SPRING, after the broker drove away, he and Stacey sat in the rented Toyota Camry and admired the house: a two-story craftsman, covered porch, plenty of character, like so many of the older houses in the neighborhood but also well-maintained. He had to admit, it was everything they'd been looking for. He even liked the color, a nice shade of blue with gray trim.

"I think we should make an offer," Stacey said.

It was raining, a drizzle that barely misted the windshield. The sky over the steeply angled roof was a watery mix of red, pink, and burnt orange, the colors blurring together like a Monet painting. Like one of *his* paintings, back in college, when he used to paint himself.

"I don't know," he said.

"Like you said, we can own it outright. We have equity in our house. And that yard!"

She looked at him. In the twilight, the interior of the car had a dusky, grainy quality, like an old filmstrip. Harsh details were lost. He could make out no crow's feet around her eyes, no silver at the roots of her red hair, no blemishes on her skin. She could have been twenty again, the age when they'd met.

"It only has one full bathroom," he said.

"Oh, we only need one full bathroom now," she

said. "If we live an hour away from John and Janey, it's not like they're going to stay with us. They'd just drive home. And who else do we need another shower for?"

"It would be better if we lived in Portland, not Rexton."

"You're the one who said we couldn't afford Portland!"

"I know, I know."

"You said our money will go farther in Rexton."

"Yes."

"The morning light in the downstairs bedroom will be so good when you start painting again."

"Oh, I doubt I'll paint anymore."

"Don't be silly! Of course you will! I saw a video the other day of a man who lost both his arms in Iraq and he paints with a brush in his mouth. If *he* can paint, you certainly can."

"Stacey—"

"And look at that yard!"

"You said that already."

"But it's so *pretty!* That cherry blossom tree will look amazing in the spring. I do so love all the green."

He felt glum. He didn't want to move to Oregon at all. He wanted to stay in L.A., but his carpal tunnel was already making it difficult to take on even the shortest freelance work, and Stacey was desperate to retire before the new mandates from the C.D.E. went into effect and forced her to rework all her lesson plans. He couldn't very well ask her to keep working. It wasn't fair.

"It's too close to the school," he said. "Traffic will be awful."

"Just twice a day, and nothing in the summer. Oh, Gavin! Think how cute a Little Free Library would look right there."

He sighed. "Not that again."

"You promised!"

"I know, I know."

"You said, when we retire—"

"Yes."

"—I can have my Little Library. And won't it look wonderful over there, on the right! There, next to the dogwood. And with the elementary school just up the road, think of all the kids who will walk by it. I'll stock it with all the children's books I've built up over the years."

"Hmm."

"I've wanted one forever!"

"I know."

"The living room will need new window furnishings."

"Of course."

"And that wallpaper in the kitchen has to go. It was ghastly."

"Yes."

She fell silent, admiring the house. As the darkness deepened, he wondered where forty years had gone. Wasn't it only yesterday when they were two

Birkenstock-clad twenty-somethings with long hair and nothing better to do than argue about the finer points of Kierkegaard? Now he couldn't remember the first thing about Kierkegaard. All he knew was that he could never deny Stacey anything. If he forgot this truism, if he hurt her or wronged her or wounded her in any way, which he often did, because he was careless and stupid about almost all things related to human feeling, the best thing to do was to apologize as soon as he realized what he had done. An apology alone was seldom enough, but it was often a good place to begin.

"I'm sorry," he said.

"For what?"

"For not getting you that Little Library sooner. We should have done it. I don't know why I fought it so much."

"Oh," she said, waving her hand dismissively and turning back to the house. But he knew it bothered her, partly because of her tone, partly because he knew she'd looked at the house so he wouldn't see her face. After forty years, he knew these things.

"I think we should make an offer," he said.

She looked at him. "Really?"

"Really."

"Oh, Gavin!"

She kissed him. A week after they moved in, they got the call from the doctor.

AFTER THE KIT ARRIVED, Gavin did not leave the house for three days. He drank his bourbon. He ate his Campbell's soup. He watched endless re-runs of all those design shows Stacey loved so much, crying like a baby when they had the big reveal, Stacey's favorite part, not knowing why he tortured himself but not being able to stop. When he walked by the crate, he just shook his head. While he'd resisted the impulse to open the box—and even more strongly resisted the impulse to bash the thing to pieces with a crowbar—he *had* looked up her Visa account and seen that she'd ordered the Little Library only a day before she'd died.

Why?

She'd known then. She'd known the end was near.

Finally, though, after three days of blubbering in self-pity, Gavin woke at 3 a.m. in a cold sweat with thoughts of the kit on his mind. He couldn't destroy it, of course. That was silly. He couldn't leave it in the house forever, either, so he might as well get on with it. He brewed a pot of coffee, drove to Home Depot as they opened and bought a six-foot cedar post and a bag of quick-drying concrete, and was outside setting the post even before the sun had fully risen over the Cascade Mountains.

He'd dug the hole and was positioning the post with a level when he heard footsteps behind him on the sidewalk. He glanced over his shoulder to see the woman with silver hair, the one who'd badgered him when the Little Library first arrived. She wore a yellow fleece coat with a matching yellow scarf.

What was her name? Fay. He offered her a polite smile and looked away, hoping that she'd leave him alone on this cold and foggy morning, but no such luck.

"Hello," she said, stopping next to him.

"Yes, hello," Gavin said.

"I see you're putting up your Little Library. I'm so glad!"

"Hmm."

"If you want any help—"

"I'm fine, thank you."

"Ah. Okay."

She started to walk away. He wiped the sweat off his brow with his shirt sleeve, watching her go, feeling bad. If his wife had seen him like this, she never would have let him hear the end of it.

"It was Stacey's idea," he said.

Fay turned, hands shoved deep in the pockets of her coat. She was short and stocky, a similar build to his wife, but of course Stacey never would have let her hair go silver like that. He'd teased her a lot about how vain it was to dye her hair red instead of letting it go natural, and she'd always shaken her head at him with a bemused smile. He wished he hadn't teased her so much.

"Stacey?" Fay asked.

"My wife."

She glanced at the dark house. "Oh, are you

setting it up so early as a surprise for her? When she wakes? How sweet of you!"

"Well . . . Not exactly, no. She, um . . . she died."

"Oh, gosh. I'm so sorry."

"She was a school teacher. She has a lot of books."

"She must have been very sweet."

"Yes."

"Are you sure you don't want any—?"

"No, no. I've got this. I just . . . I wanted you to know, that's all."

"Okay."

"So, um, I'll get back to it here."

"Right."

She fidgeted with her yellow scarf. "You know, I walk a lot. If you ever . . . you know, want to go for a walk sometime . . ."

"Oh."

"I'm a good listener. I'm alone, too . . . Well, divorced after 34 years, so I—I can't, you know—"

"Ah."

"—understand completely. But still. I understand, you know, the . . . the emptiness. How something feels missing."

"Sure."

"If you ever . . ."

"Yes. Maybe. I'm, um, I'm going to finish this now. I'll, uh, I'll let you know about that."

"Okay. See you around?"

"Sure, sure."

She smiled furtively before walking away, but he

could see the disappointment in her eyes, the dashed hope. She had nice teeth. Very pretty. But what could he tell her? He wasn't going to walk with her, that was ridiculous. He was going to finish this silly Little Library, stock it with the children's books boxed up in the attic, and then he would sit in a dark room, sit so still that maybe he could feel the Earth turning on its axis, ignore the phone, hope John didn't come down again to check on him and be an overall nuisance.

He'd get this done, forget about it, watch stupid shows about people flipping houses and houses flipping on people or something equally inane and eat his soup and drink his bourbon and hopefully he wouldn't have to talk to anyone about anything for a very long time.

That was the plan. Yet the next morning, Fay knocked on his door.

"YOU NEED BOOKS," Fay said.

"What?"

"In your Little Library. It's empty."

It was Sunday and the street was quiet, the air heavy with moisture under an overcast sky. This time, Gavin was dressed—just jeans and a white T-shirt, but at least he wasn't wearing a bathrobe. Fay stood on his porch, wearing a bright green rain slicker, a shopping bag from Safeway slung over her shoulder. Even in the overcast light, her eyes shone brightly and her silver hair, against her green vinyl jacket, glimmered like tinsel on a Christmas tree. He could just make out a loaf of Franz bread sticking out the top of her bag. The rhododendron next to his door, whose red blooms had only just opened in the last day, glistened from the night's rain.

Gavin peered around her at the Little Library. He couldn't make out the interior from this angle, but the library itself, made to resemble a blue craftsman just like his house, seemed fine. The quick-setting concrete had kept the cedar post perfectly level.

"Already?" he said. "I just stocked it last night."

"What time?"

"At least a dozen children's books."

He walked to the sidewalk in his bare feet, the concrete cold and damp.

"You should get shoes," Fay said, following him.

"It was right before dark," Gavin said. "How many people could actually walk by between then and now?"

"My daughter likes to walk outside barefoot, too," Fay said. "I'm always afraid she's going to step on broken glass."

Sure enough, when Gavin got to the Little Library, he could see there was nothing inside. He opened the glass door anyway and felt around on the platform; the painted plywood was cool but dry. What did he think he was going to find? A hole the books fell through? He looked up and down the street, saw no one. A crow peered down at him from the telephone wire.

Gavin turned to Fay abruptly. "Are you messing with me?" he asked.

"What?"

"Is this a joke?"

"A joke? What do you mean?"

"A practical joke. Did you take the books?"

"What?"

"It's okay if you did. Ha, ha. You got me. What, is someone recording this? You have a friend in the bushes over there?"

She stared at him. "Wait, you think . . . You think *I* stole your books?"

"Well, I didn't say *stole*. I think it was more like a—"

"How could you think that?" Her eyes misted. They were big eyes, so it was quite the misting, and he felt terrible. "What an awful thing to say!"

"Listen, it was just a—"

"Children's books, too! Why—why would I do such a thing? Excuse me. Excuse me, I have to go."

She hurried away.

NOTHING like that happened again for two weeks. Gavin restocked the children's books. He didn't see Fay either, though he wasn't sure he would have been able to muster the courage to talk to her even if he had.

He checked the Little Library each night. Some days nothing changed. Other days a few of the children's books were gone, replaced with others, old Grishams, dog-eared Nora Roberts, a Mediterranean cookbook that he flipped through himself, thinking how much Stacey had loved baklava, until his mind drifted back to the twenty-year anniversary trip they'd taken to Greece. They'd talked about going back for their fortieth. Something else that wouldn't happen.

As the cherry blossom tree outside his window exploded into full bloom, then, after only a couple weeks, began to litter the sidewalk with pink petals until all the branches were bare, the Little Library operated the way it was supposed to. When he was in his kitchen and had a clear view of it, he saw people taking books, leaving books, and perusing books without taking or leaving, and that was fine, it made him sad that Stacey wasn't here to see it, but it was fine that it was out there. He'd done it.

But then when he was buttering toast one misty morning, he saw a blond boy on his way to school stop in front of the Little Library. He took off his backpack, removed what looked like a Hardy Boys book, and opened the Little Library's door.

Instead of putting his book inside, however, the boy peered within for a long time, shook his head, and put his book back in his bag. Then he walked away.

Mystified, Gavin went out to check for himself. Sure enough, the Little Library was empty again.

He restocked with another load of children's books from the attic, but this time he was concerned enough that he started checking each night. Four days later, it was again empty. Annoyed, he restocked. Then only two days passed before they were gone. He restocked again and sat there until nearly midnight, watching the damn thing, saw nothing.

Yet in the morning, it was empty.

He called the police. They did nothing, and worse, he felt embarrassed for calling them in the first place. Yes, they were free books, but that wasn't the point, was it? That wasn't the point at all.

Stacey would understand.

Stacey would understand if she were here.

IT WENT LIKE THAT, on and off, the books there some mornings, gone others, until finally Gavin couldn't take it anymore. He brewed his coffee, situated himself in the dark by the kitchen window, and vowed to stay up all night, every night, until he managed to catch the wretched Little Library thief himself.

It was on the fourth night, one of the foggiest

they'd had in a while, that Gavin finally saw something unusual. A short, shapely woman in a dark sweatshirt stopped around one in the morning to peer inside the Little Free Library box. Gavin sat up in his chair. The street, bustling during the day, was so still that the hum of his refrigerator sounded like a lion's roar. She glanced left, right, the hood shadowing her face completely, then reached inside her jacket and pulled out a cloth shopping bag.

"Ah!" Gavin cried.

Stupid. It was an involuntary response. He'd yelled so loudly that she actually looked at his window. The fog was too thick and the shadows too deep for him to make out her face, but there was no doubt she'd heard him.

This was what got him. She could have run. He probably would have let her go, figuring shame would have kept her from returning. But no. Instead she actually had the gall to still reach into the library and scoop out all the children's books before calmly walking away.

He bolted out of the house to catch her. No more than a few seconds had passed before Gavin reached the sidewalk. It wasn't fast enough. He saw the woman a block away, hustling around the corner onto Oak Street. Cursing, he sprinted after her.

The thick air dampened his face. The tennis shoes were tight and stiff; it was another thing Stacey had bought for him from Amazon that he had not yet worn. In the yellow glow from the streetlamp, the cherry blossom petals littering the sidewalk reminded him of the rose petals Stacey's mother had sprinkled on the church steps the day of their wedding.

He'd never been much of a runner, but now he was absolutely dreadful, like he was submerged in water. Even after one block, his lungs burned. When he reached the corner, gasping for breath, he looked north down Oak. The thief was now *two* blocks away. She was past the elementary school and rounding onto Lincoln.

He bent over, hands on his knees. He might have given up right there, probably *would* have given up right there, since he didn't see how he could ever catch her, when it occurred to him that this might be the very same woman he'd felt terrible about accusing earlier.

Fay.

Why not? The woman's build was about right. Perhaps her mortified reaction, when he'd asked if she'd taken the books, had all been an act. Maybe she was some kind of bibliophile kleptomaniac, emptying little libraries everywhere, hoarding them in her house, causing untold suffering to children all over the city.

Deep down, Gavin knew his suspicion might not be justified, but it was enough to get him off and running again. He dashed past Lockley Elementary, past swing sets and monkey bars and netless basketball hoops, all coated in fog as thick as stretched cotton balls, and he remembered how Stacey had talked about how they might bring grandchildren here someday, if John and Janey ever got around to having them. "Just like we used to take John to the one near our house," she'd said, wistfully.

Something inside Gavin was breaking. He could feel it breaking. When he turned onto Lincoln, he saw the woman three blocks to the east, rounding onto Whitley, and he almost gave into the hopelessness then, the despair, but no. He wouldn't. He would keep running until his lungs collapsed, until his heart smashed through his ribcage, and until his legs gave out from under him. Catch her or die. There was no alternative.

She was three blocks away now —*three!*—and almost to Barnaby Park. If she disappeared into the sprawling, oak-filled park, he'd never catch her. It may have been a finely-landscaped city park during the day, full of playgrounds, jogging tracks, and even the Rexton College athletic field, but at night it became a dark and forbidding forest except for a single, solitary lighted trail that led from the south side to the north.

Gavin ran. His neck felt slick with sweat; his shirt, under his sweatshirt, stuck to his skin like plastic wrap. Logic dictated he had no chance to reach her, she was way too far ahead and increasing her lead, but a strange thing happened when she got to the edge of the park.

She stopped.

Ahead of her, the tops of the oak trees, spindly and leafless, caught the fringes of the light from the streetlamps. He jogged another block, not sure what she was doing, and not sure what *he* would do, either, if he actually caught her, but then his lungs just couldn't take it anymore. He stopped, bent over, choking in the thick air. She was two blocks away, but she might as well have been two miles.

Yet she didn't leave. She simply stood there, staring into the tapestry of oaks that vanished into the gloom. He started walking. Still she didn't move. There were houses on both sides, mostly old Craftsmans, Victorians, and colonials, a neighborhood of unique houses much like his own. Most of them had lighted windows and TVs aglow and a few people here and there inside, moving about, but there was nobody on the street between him and the Little Library thief. Another block and he'd reach her.

That was when the woman put her arm up.

He stopped. At first, he thought maybe she was waving to someone in the park, but then he realized she might also have been signaling him to stop. But why?

He caught movement to his left.

There was a small white Victorian with two dormered windows. The curtains in the living room were open and he could see inside even though a white sheen made the details fuzzy. There, sitting in a rocking chair reading a coffee table-sized book, was a woman with silver hair. He blinked the sweat out of his eyes and saw that it wasn't just any woman.

It was Fay.

She wore a pink shawl over her shoulders, the same color as the cherry blossom petals spotting the lighted path to her front door. She was engrossed in her book and didn't notice him. As she turned the page—it was an art book, maybe even one on Monet, judging by the bright pastels—Gavin felt remorse not just for how he'd treated her before, but how he'd suspected her now.

He looked back at the Little Library thief and saw that the woman had started walking. She wasn't heading left, toward the trail, but directly into the forest. She was disappearing into the gloom. In a second, she'd be gone.

"Wait," he said.

It came out as a choked whisper, certainly not loud enough for her to hear, but she stopped anyway. She turned her head, but not all the way around, just enough that he saw that some of her hair had come out of her hoodie. It was dark, but she stood in such a way that the hair caught the light from the last lamp on the last street before the park.

Red.

Red hair.

There was no mistake. As the woman kept walking into the trees, it finally occurred to Gavin who he'd been chasing. His rational mind dismissed it as nonsense, it couldn't be, such a thing was impossible, the woman's build, the color of her hair, it was all just coincidence, but still, he knew. He also knew he had a choice. He could follow her into the darkness—until his lungs collapsed, until his legs gave out from under him—or he could let her go.

Feeling something tearing inside him, he turned toward the old Victorian. Fay was still reading. Would she mind? It was half past eight. It wasn't too late, was it? He walked across the cherry blossom petals. He stepped onto the porch. He raised his hand to the door. What would he say? What could he possibly say?

He looked one last time toward the park. The woman was almost gone. He could just make out the shape of her. A smudge of darkness under the oaks. She wasn't stopping. He wasn't going after her—and then, turning back to the door, he knew what to say.

He'd start by saying he was sorry. An apology alone was seldom enough, but it was often a good place to begin.

CREATIVE VICE

It was Rick's idea. Spend a week doing ride-alongs with a cop friend of his, a good way to get acquainted with the city. That I was originally from Rexton, that Rick, of all people, knew this full well, having been my friend since we met the first day of high school in Mrs. Martin's creative writing class, not two miles from where we both sat, did not dissuade him at all.

"Yeah, but I *know* you, Chris," he said, after I argued that I was hardly new to town. "You've been in California a long time—what, fifteen years? You don't think like a writer who lives in Oregon anymore."

We were sitting in his office and it was raining so hard I could barely hear him over the splatter on the concrete patio. It smelled like printer toner and burnt coffee. The brass clock on the wall read half past eight and only a few people remained in the newsroom outside his office.

It was a cold November Wednesday, a couple months before a pandemic started raging across the country and a year before Trump was ousted from office.

"I come back every Christmas!" I protested. My socks were soaked and my toes were numb and it brought back everything I didn't like about living in Rexton. "You know that. We even have dinner sometimes. I know this town."

"We haven't had dinner in years."

"Oh, come on. It was just last December."

Chuckling, he jotted a name and number down on a yellow sticky note, which he handed to me. "His name is Tom Brady. *Not* the football player, obviously. And don't mention that. It's kind of a sore subject for him, especially since he's a huge Seahawks fan. Look, it's just a week. You may be from Rexton, but you've never worked the crime beat here."

"I worked it at the Los Angeles Times. It's just a tiny bit bigger, you know." I held my fingers an inch apart.

He ran a hand through his black hair, not nearly as much hair as I remembered, and not nearly so black, so he may have been right about how long it'd been since we'd had dinner. "Yeah, but how long ago was that? You didn't work for the paper long. You were doing your Hollywood thing a long time before you … well, you know."

I nodded, feeling my cheeks burn. I hated that he saw me this way, as some kind of charity case, as a burnt-out husk of the guy he once knew. I wanted to keep arguing, but I knew I couldn't. He'd never insist, he'd never tell me this was an order, not a request, but I could see in his eyes that it was.

"It's just a week," he said.

"Okay."

"Be good for you."

"Right."

He chuckled. "Don't screw this up, Chris."

"What?"

"Nothing. Just messing with you. How's Amy, by the way? She find work yet? You know, my wife's cousin is a dentist in Silverton. He might be able to hook her up."

I stared at him, trying to keep myself from sprinting out of the room to take the elevator down three floors, a big building by Rexton standards, and hustling through the rainy windswept streets until I found a dingy bar where they'd never tell me I'd had too much. *Just messing with you.* But he wasn't. He was deadly serious. And Amy? Jesus, that was not someplace I wanted to go, even with him.

Don't screw this up, Chris.

I looked at the sticky note. "I'll call him tomorrow," I said.

"METH IS the big problem in Rexton," Tom Brady said, as we rattled over the rails on 13th street. "I mean, it's the big problem everywhere, right, but it's really bad here in the Willamette Valley. We thought we'd beaten it back twenty years ago and now it's back with a vengeance—all that cheap Mexican meth flooding our streets. And almost all the low-level crime is because of the Tweakers."

He shot me a glance, as if trying to see if I might be offended. In the dark patrol car, his ruddy face was awash in shadows, his uniform badge glinting blue in the glow from his dashboard computer. He was a huge guy, bulky, with the kind of thick neck that made me think of the heavyweight fighter Mike Tyson. That was a good description for him. Like a white Mike Tyson. He didn't look anything like Tom Brady the football player.

It was a week after I'd started at the *Register*. We'd only barely left the station's parking garage but my back was already killing me. Mercifully, it was no longer raining, a drizzly stretch that had lasted over five days, but the temperature had also dropped enough that I'd slipped on a patch of ice coming out of Mom's house that evening. If my back hurt this bad after only a few minutes in the seat, I couldn't imagine riding around with him for a week.

"Right, the Tweakers," I said, jotting a note in my spiral notebook to make him feel like I was taking him seriously. I'd never done meth, booze was more my thing, but I'd tried just about everything else at least once. He'd been talking nonstop since we shook hands but it was all I could do not to think about how good a few drinks would make my back feel. "You think maybe we can pick up some coffee at some point?"

"Oh, sure," he said, "we'll get some from the county lockup. See, a lot of people think it's the homeless committing the crimes, and the numbers don't lie, but most of the homeless are either mentally ill or drug addicts, so it's all related. That's why I'm not a big fan of people trying to decriminalize drugs, like the bill that just passed here in Oregon. Sure, these people need treatment, but it's hard to stop drug-related crime if we're telling people drugs are okay."

I knew I shouldn't argue, it was going to be a long week if I made things tense, but I couldn't help myself. "Well, Portugal did something similar back in 2000," I said. "And they didn't find that drug use or drug-related crime increased."

"Portugal?" he said. "Oregon isn't Portugal. You're spending too much time with those California liberals. Didn't Rick say you grew up in Los Angeles?"

"Actually, I grew up in Rexton," I said. I almost added, *a few blocks from here,* but I wasn't sure I wanted Officer Brady to know I grew up in the area locals called Felony Flats. He might think I was a Tweaker, too … which I guess I was, of a sort. Instead I laughed and, hoping to change the subject, said, "It has been a while, though. It's why Rick thought this would be a good idea. I appreciate it, by the way."

Brady waved his hand as if it was no big deal.

"Well, I'm sure a lot has changed. Rick said you directed some movies or something. Anything I would know?"

"Screenplays, actually."

"What's that?"

Inside my leather jacket, my phone buzzed. I didn't look. I knew who it was, the same person who'd been calling, texting, and emailing me the past two weeks. Amy. Always Amy, my girlfriend of almost five years, the one who'd seen both my meteoric rise and my rapid fall.

Of all the mirrors that reflected back my own failure, looking into Amy's eyes had been the most revealing—and the hardest to bear. She believed in me when no one else did. She said I'd always be unhappy unless I was doing something really creative, and I just needed to get my foot in the door with Hollywood again. She'd even gotten me a job offer. One of her patients, a woman who adored Amy as most of her patients did, was the showrunner on *Joey Knows!,* a Nickelodeon production about a teenage girl who could read minds, and this woman said she'd hire me to be a staff writer. As a favor to Amy, of course.

I told Amy I'd rather go back to journalism than work for a brain-dead sitcom with an exclamation point in the title and a laugh track for an audience too stupid to know when to chuckle on their own. She said I was being elitist and that I was going to be miserable unless I was working as a screenwriter.

She said I might be able to lie to her, Rick, everybody, but not to myself.

What I didn't tell her was that I knew she was right, but the real problem was I couldn't bear the thought of standing at the foot of the mountain again, and a staff writer on *Joey Knows!* was definitely at the bottom of the mountain. Every day I toiled there would be a reminder of how far I'd fallen.

And so I ran, as far from that mountain as I could get, back to Rexton, back to my mother's, called Rick, convinced him to hire me even though he really didn't have the budget for it.

"I'm a writer," I said to Officer Brady. "I write screenplays. Or at least, I did. Now I'm a journalist again."

"Oh yeah? Tells you what I know. I thought the director wrote the movie."

I laughed. "Some directors do. They change the scripts so much you wouldn't even think they're yours. I was lucky, though, at least with my first movie. What you saw on screen was pretty much what I wrote. You ever seen *The Pact?* It starred Tag Deerhorn and K.C. McIntire? About a group of teenagers who kill a bully who was terrorizing one of them?"

I looked at him. We were passing under a streetlamp, so it was easy enough to see his face, and I could tell right away that he didn't. "Maybe," he said. "I think ... Yeah, I might have caught it on HBO a couple years ago. There was a teacher that came back as a zombie, right?"

I grimaced. "Actually, that was *Teacher's Pet*. A different movie."

"Oh, right! Yeah, that was a good one."

"It was, yeah. I think it was a Steven Crown adaptation. I don't think he wrote it, though. I think it was adapted by—"

"Had me right up to the end! I mean, having the teacher come back from the dead and, like, take over the dog's mind. That was something!"

"Yeah."

"So you wrote that?"

"No, no. That was Steven Crown. I mean, it was based on one of his novellas."

"What's a novella?"

"Well, it's ... it's a short novel."

"Why don't they call it that, then?"

"I ... I don't know, actually. Maybe because that's two words instead of one?"

"Oh. Yeah." He chuckled and tapped the steering wheel. "Good one there, Carpenter. Rick said you were funny. Real quick, he said."

"Sure."

"What else you write?"

I almost said *Faraway and Forever,* because I knew he'd know it, everybody knew that movie, and some part of me wanted to impress good old Officer Brady, but even so, I couldn't bring myself to do it. It wasn't my movie. I wrote the original script, I'd been paid a hell of a lot of money for it, but so many other screenwriters had a go at it that by the time it actually got into Mr. Bigshot Director's hands there was hardly anything left of my original story except the title.

And of course that was the one that went on to become a blockbuster and get nominated for a slew of awards, just narrowly missing the Best Picture Oscar that year, which was a good thing. If it had actually won, I might have killed myself instead of going on a two-week bender that was really the beginning of my fast track descent into Hell. And eventually rehab. And eventually here, in Rexton, riding shotgun next to good old Officer Brady.

"Oh, I wrote a few things," I said, "but not a lot was produced. Got paid well, though."

"What do you mean it wasn't produced?"

"I mean, it wasn't made. Happens all the time in Hollywood."

"You mean, you get paid for writing something even if no one makes it?"

"Yeah. Actually, that's true of almost all screenwriters, even most of the very successful ones."

"Huh. Just seems weird, getting paid if no movie was actually made."

"Well, we still do the work."

"I guess. It just seems like, you know, if a writer wrote a book but didn't actually make it into a book, a real book, then they wouldn't expect to get paid, you know? If it was just sitting on their computer. You see what I'm saying?"

My face felt warm, and I heard the tension in my voice as I grew defensive. "We do a lot of rewrites, too. Something's not quite working in a script, they bring in another writer to fix it. Only a tiny fraction of scripts actually get greenlit by a studio, and even then, things fall apart, or they can't get the actors they want, or … There's a million reasons. If you write it completely on spec, of course, you don't get paid, but there's not many screenwriters that can afford to do that. Got bills to pay, you know."

"Sure, I get it."

But he didn't. I doubted he even knew what *on spec* meant, and that was fine, I didn't need to explain myself to Officer Brady, especially since I was a journalist now, not a screenwriter.

Yet for some reason I still felt the need to impress him. He was looking at the road, scanning the tract houses with the flaking paint, the chain link fences infested with ivy and junipers, and the occasional tireless car up on cinderblocks, the part of town Mom and I lived in after dad took off when I was three. This was before Mom married an estate lawyer just after I fled for California, a guy who died just a few years back, leaving her everything including the house that abutted Shady Oaks Golf Course. A nice place. A much better life. Not my kind of place, but nice, and good for her.

But this part of town, where I now rumbled over

the potholes with Officer Brady? Felony Flats would always be my childhood. It was a black hole exerting its gravitational pull on me. I wanted Brady to know that I'd achieved escape velocity once, and maybe, after I got my feet under me, I would so again.

"You ever see *Faraway and Forever?*" I asked him.

His eyes lit up. "Oh sure! *Everybody* has seen that movie. Wow! Cooper Coleman was amazing. You wrote that?"

"I did," I said, and I should have left it at that, but I couldn't help myself. There was still some part of me that just couldn't take credit for words that weren't mine: "The original script, anyway."

"The original script?"

"Yeah. It went through some changes."

"How many changes?"

"You know. Rewrites. Normal stuff."

Brady laughed. "That had some great lines in it. I remember when Cooper, you know as the sheriff, he chased the bad guy into the library, looks right at the dude and says, 'If you want to check out a book, you'll need your library card.' And then, *pow!* He shoots him right through that encyclopedia."

"Yeah."

"That was good stuff! The look on the sheriff's face. You wrote that, right?"

"Um … No, not that line."

"Oh. But you came up with the library part?"

"Well … Actually, I had that scene set in a coffee shop. But there was still a shootout—"

"A coffee shop?"

"Yeah."

"I don't know how the library card line would work if it was in a coffee shop. Were there books in the coffee shop?"

"No. But, the way I wrote it—"

"What about the scene where he hid under the bed when the bad guy's girlfriend gives birth and there's like ten mob guys in the room with machine guns? You wrote that?" Brady slapped his knee. "Man! That was some seriously funny shit. That was yours, right?"

I was about to say *no*, because I didn't, of course I didn't, there was hardly anything in that piece of crap that was mine. Yet something about being in that patrol car with the heaters running full bore and the shadows in Officer Brady's eyes and the crappy neighborhood I grew up in passing by the windows, abandoned shopping carts, rusty bikes, a cat pawing through a garbage can, it was all there, the horror of my youth, I felt something break inside me, a little thing, like a thread that was keeping my integrity from falling into the dark void at the center of me where everything else had gone. It snapped and that was it.

"Yeah," I said. "Yeah, I wrote that. Good stuff, huh?"

"It sure was! It was awesome!"

"Thanks."

"But why are you here?"

"What's that?"

"I mean, back in Rexton. You write something that good, I figure you should be living in a big mansion in California. Why are you back in Oregon?"

"Well—"

"Oh, crap. It's Bigfoot."

"Bigfoot?"

"There's a warrant out for him—parole violation. I gotta bring him in."

As he swerved the cruiser to the side of the road, I thought maybe he was making a joke. *Ha, ha, let's arrest Sasquatch.* Even when I saw the shirtless hairy guy on a bicycle coming our way, I still thought Brady was messing with me. The guy really *did* look like Bigfoot, he was so hairy. In fact, when I first saw him, I thought maybe he was wearing a fur coat, the hair on his chest was so dark and thick.

He was broad-shouldered, too, just as I would have expected Bigfoot to be, but as soon as he was closer I saw that there was no depth to him; turn him sideways and there was more hair to him than skin and bones. He had what Amy called "the Jesus look," although a very unhealthy version of one, his face disappearing inside an unruly brown beard and an oily mane that both clumped and scattered, like dreadlocks coming undone.

His tight jeans had holes in the knees and mud stains all over the legs. He was barefoot, and his enormous feet, like hairy snowshoes, could barely stay on the bike's pedals. The bike was a kid's bike, way too small for him, and the style, with that long yellow banana seat, was one I hadn't seen since I was a kid. He bobbed and weaved as he rode, and it was any wonder he didn't fall off, he looked so off balance.

Only when Brady put the cruiser in park and partly opened his door did I realize he wasn't joking. The guy on the bicycle was still half a block away, but he slowed when he saw the police car.

"You stay put while I arrest him," Brady said, keeping his gaze fixed on Bigfoot. "Damn idiot—this is the third time I've arrested him this year. Last time was for exposing himself to a woman at the 7-11. Can you believe that shit?"

Brady stepped outside, cold air blasting into the cruiser before he slammed the door. The guy on the bike had already gotten off, stumbling onto the weedy area near a crumpling Winnebago covered by a blue tarp. Brady approached him with one hand up, one hand on his holster. They were about the same height, but Bigfoot was probably half the weight. A shaggy beanpole.

Bigfoot looked at the Winnebago, as if thinking about diving inside. I gripped the armrest, my heart rate kicking up a notch. I'd been on plenty of ride-alongs over the years, so I should have been used to this sort of thing by now, but no matter how many times I saw an officer confronting a perp, it never got old. There was always the possibility of something big happening—a fight, a shooting, something.

But, like usual, there was just some animated talking, then the two of them walked back to the cruiser. Brady didn't even cuff him. He just opened the back door and directed him into the seat, which Bigfoot fell into, arms and legs bending in all sorts of weird ways. I was separated from him by a wire mesh.

"I can't leave my bike," Bigfoot was saying, as cold air again rushed into the cruiser. "I can't just leave it here, man, somebody might steal it."

I knew that voice.

That was my first thought. For a guy so big, one might have expected a low, Charlton Heston-like rumble, but this one was nasally and high, kind of weaselly. I tried to discern his face through that swarm of hair, but all I could see was a flash of dark eyes and grimy skin. I didn't recognize him. He was bobbing his head as if in tune to a song only he could hear, looking up at Brady. He smelled like marijuana, beer, and Chinese food all at once.

"I'm sure it will be fine," Brady said. "That thing's not worth five bucks."

"No, no, no, man, I can't leave it. Can't you throw it in the trunk?"

"It won't fit. Sorry."

"Aw, man. Can't you, like, put it in my place? It's only down the street here. See the yellow house. I live above the garage, man. Can't you just put it inside? I don't want nobody to steal it."

"Bruce," I said.

I said the name even as it popped into my head. They both looked at me. Bigfoot—or the guy I'd known in high school as Bruce Garwood—brushed his mop of hair away from his face and leaned toward the mesh. His face was gaunt and covered with the kind of thick grime found at the bottom of a tub, but I saw the Bruce I'd known under the mask of his misery.

"Chris?" he said. "Chris Carpenter, that you, man? Shit, I can't believe it."

"You *know* him?" Brady said.

"Yeah, yeah," Bruce said. "We like went to high school together. Shit, man, it's been like forever. Jesus, what are you doing here? Man, we had some good times back then, didn't we? It's *good* to see you!"

I was at a loss for words, something that rarely happened to me. They used to call him Bruce "Bigfoot" Garwood, not because he resembled the mythical beast but because he literally had size fourteen feet. Those huge natural flippers, when paired with his long arms and broad shoulders, came in handy in the pool. He'd been a star swimmer, anchoring a state championship both his junior and senior years, which also landed him a full-ride scholarship to Yale. Some people even thought he might have had a shot at the Olympics.

He'd also been a raging asshole.

At least to me. And to Ricky. And to any of the people who hadn't been part of the peppy popular crowd. To call me a friend was laughable. He'd been two years ahead of us and I still had a vivid memory of him picking me up when I was a freshman and shoving me into a locker. Even after I'd interviewed him for the student newspaper, he could never remember my name.

"Hey, man," I said.

"Wow!" Bruce said. "It's like a blast from the past! I heard you went on to make movies like Steven Spielberg, man! That's so awesome!"

It was a strange feeling, knowing Bruce "Bigfoot" Garwood had heard about me. I should have felt vindicated, I suppose, but I didn't. I just felt sad.

Right then, my phone buzzed again. It had to be Amy. It was her modus operandi, after all. She always called ten minutes after the first attempt, but she never left a message the second time. In the tight space, the sound was loud enough that it made Bruce jump.

"Who's that?" he asked.

"Oh, just … nobody, really."

Bruce laughed. "Probably Stephen Spielberg, right? You should take it. He wants you to help make the sequel to ET."

"No, no, nobody like that," I said. Then, I don't know why, but I added, "It's just my girlfriend Amy. She's—she's still in L.A. She's just, you know, checking up on me."

"Oh, is she like an actress? I bet she's a hot actress, right?"

"All right, you two," Brady said, "I hate to break up this little high school reunion, but I still have to arrest Bruce. But I'm sure you'll be released tonight, it just being a parole violation."

"I didn't really miss my meeting," Bruce said. "It's a misunderstanding is all."

"Yeah, well, you can take that up with the judge. But I'll tell you what I'm going to do, I'll put your bike in your apartment for you, okay? I can at least do that. As long as you're giving me permission?"

"Yeah, yeah, that would be great! Key is under the Buddha statue."

"Okay," Brady said. "Come on, Hollywood. Regulations don't allow me to leave you in the car with him, so you got to come with me. You want to call your girlfriend on the way, that's fine."

"No, no, " I said, "it's nothing urgent."

Reluctantly, I got out of the car, Bruce excitedly thanking both of us as if we were doing him a favor. I was still kicking myself for mentioning Amy.

My breath fogged in front of my face. Brady took his bike and wheeled it toward the yellow house, me laboring just behind, trying not to limp. I heard a man and a woman arguing in a house across the street. An old woman sat smoking on a covered porch. Televisions lit up almost all of the windows with a flickering blue glow. I smelled moldy leaves, grilling hamburgers from the bar on 12th, and chimney smoke.

"You guys were really friends, huh?" Brady asked.

"What?" I said. "No, no, not really."

"Then why did he—"

"I don't know why he said it. I mean, we were classmates, but that was it. I didn't really know him."

"Oh. Hey, you know, I was thinking about what you said. About doing your writing and getting paid but not having the stuff made."

"Yeah?" I felt queasy even going down this conversational road again.

"Yeah, I just wanted to say I was thinking it was kind of like me."

"How so?"

"Just that I arrest a lot of guys, guys like Bigfoot, and it's just a revolving door, you know? They're right back on the street doing the same crap. Feels kind of pointless sometimes. But I just do my best, you know? That's all I can do. If I do my job the best I can, I figure that's enough, right? Kind of like you with the writing, even if nothing gets made. Here, help me carry the bike up the stairs."

I didn't know what to say in response to his comment, so I was glad we'd reached Bruce's place. The wooden stairs behind the garage were slick and coated with leaves, so we had to be careful. I was in so much pain that sweat broke out on my brow, but I wasn't about to wimp out on Officer Brady. I realized, as I gripped the rusty metal bar behind the banana seat, that he didn't know Bruce "Bigfoot" Garwood's real history, or the bright future that once lay before him. To Brady, this was what Bruce was, where he belonged.

Something occurred to me. There might have been a story for the *Rexton Register* in this, a "whatever happened to" feature about the fallen golden boy, a tragic Icarus-like tale of flying too close to the sun. Something. I'd find the angle. There had to be a hell of a story to explain how the son of a heart surgeon, who lived up on Sunridge Drive with all the other one-percenters, had ended up shirtless in the back of a patrol car with nobody knowing who he was.

The stone Buddha statue was at the top of the stairs, in the corner. Brady, leading the way with one hand on the front wheel, put down his end of the bike and found the key. He unlocked the door and then we were inside—a one-room flat with a dirty kitchen, a Murphy bed, and the rest of the room packed with the kind of musty, seaweed-colored furniture that wouldn't have made the cut even at the Salvation Army thrift shop. It smelled like booze and sweat and day-old pizza and a million other odors that hit both of us like an olfactory eighteen wheeler.

"Dear God," Brady said, "the dude should open a window once in a while ... Oh, crap."

"What?"

He pointed at what amounted to a coffee table, a wooden door propped up by a pair of five-gallon paint drums. On top was a Buck Rogers TV tray, coated with fine white powder and a plastic bag filled with the stuff. "That's meth," Brady said. "Now I gotta book him for possession, too. Since he invited me in, it's totally admissible." He shook his head at me. "If he'd just put the crap away, I never would have seen it. I'm afraid your little reunion with your friend will have to wait. He'll be in jail at least overnight."

"Like I said, he's not my friend," I said.

"Too bad this didn't happen in January."

"What do you mean?"

"That law I told you about, the one that just passed — he'd just have to pay a $100 fine instead of going to jail." Brady laughed. "Dude just can't catch a break. Man, timing is everything isn't it?"

THREE DAYS LATER, after another long evening shuttling around town with Officer Brady, I knocked on Bruce's door. Nobody answered. It was a clear Friday night, even colder than before, and the leaves sticking to his stairs gleamed with newly-formed ice. My mom's red Mustang was parked along the street, lit up under a streetlamp where I could clearly see it.

I tried knocking again. Still no answer. I knew from the police blotter that he'd been let out on Wednesday. I tried a third time, waited a long time in the frigid cold, then finally started back down the stairs. I was almost there when I heard the screech of brakes and then there he was, pulling to a stop just as his front bicycle tire banged into a metal garbage can.

He looked up at me, face shrouded by all that hair, eyes gleaming in the moonlight like someone peeking out of a bush. He was wearing a shirt this time, a bright yellow Hawaiian number, and black Nike exercise tights that had a hole in the right knee. He had a brown paper sack rolled up under one arm, and when he saw me, he tucked the bag closer to his body.

"Hey, man," I said.

Inside that cloud of hair, I saw him blink. "Cary send you? I'll pay him in a week, I promise."

"No, it's me, Chris Carpenter. Don't you remember? We met in Officer Brady's car on Tuesday—or re-met, I guess."

"Oh!" he said, relaxing his shoulders. "Oh, Chris! Yeah, that's right! What're you doing here, man? You come to shoot the breeze, talk about old times?"

"I tried calling," I said, "but the line was disconnected."

"Oh, man, sorry about that. I guess I forgot to pay the bill. That's okay, though. I'm glad you just stopped by. You want to come in? It's so good to see you, man!"

"You want some help with your bike?"

"No, no, I got it, man. Just be careful cause all the ice. That your ride down there? Shit, that's a nice car. My dad had a Mustang once."

I wasn't about to admit it was my mom's car. "I remember your dad having a lot of nice cars," I said. "Didn't you drive to school in a Corvette sometimes?"

"Yeah, yeah, a '67. That was a truly sweet ride, man. He even gave it to me in the will. Shit, I wished I still had it. But I had to pay the rent, you know?"

There was a lot to unpack in what he just said, a whole story, really, and I felt myself getting more excited about all the different angles I could take. Golden boy athlete goes to Yale, Dad dies, boy's life goes down the drain, turns to drugs, ends up here … As I followed him into the apartment, I debated about where to start, and realized that I hadn't even told him why I was there.

"Hey Bruce, one thing," I said, closing the door behind us. The room looked just as disheveled but it smelled even worse, as if there was a toilet somebody had forgotten to flush. "I'm actually here for two reasons. One, just to say hi, but two, because I might like to write a story about you."

Bruce brightened. "Oh yeah? Like a movie?"

"Well … Right now I'm thinking a feature in the *Rexton Register.* I'm a journalist now, you know, and—"

"I think it would make a great movie." He bobbed his way into the kitchen, more bounce in his step as his voice rose. "I mean, there's a lot of twists and turns in my life, man. If I were you, I'd like, you know, take some creative vice so you can go forward and put a happy ending on it."

"License."

"What?"

"Creative license. I think that's what you meant."

"What'd I say?"

"Creative vice."

"Did I?" He laughed. "That's funny. Creative vice. Man, see, I'm interesting even when I don't try to be. That's like you, man. You're a screenwriter. It's your creative vice. You're hooked on it." He moved some plastic containers full of something moldy and rotten. As thin as he was, he was still a big guy, and there was a jittery looseness to him that made me feel like he might knock something over at any moment. "But yeah, man, whatever. You working for the paper, huh?"

"That's right."

"And you want to hear *my* story?"

"I do."

"Like right now?"

"Like right now."

He clapped his hands. "All *riiiight!* Let's get to it. You want some coffee? Water? Milk? Wait, the milk is spoiled. I might have some tea ..."

I told him I was fine. He poured himself a glass of water and settled into a camping chair, one near a television I hadn't even seen because there was a print of the Mona Lisa on its side in front of it. Someone had inked a big handlebar mustache on Mona Lisa with a black marker. He directed me toward the seaweed couch, and when I sat in it, I kept on sitting, my rear end sinking until my knees nearly touched my chin.

I asked him if I could record him on my iPhone.

He told me that was fine. I took out a spiral notepad to jot some notes. He was talking before I even got my pen out, starting his story when he arrived at Yale. It was all going well, he said, until a few weeks in there was a girl who led him on at a frat party but then claimed he raped her. His dad got a lawyer and it was going to go to court, where Bruce insisted he would have been proven innocent, but then she agreed to accept a financial settlement to drop the charges. It was all very hush hush, but Bruce felt vindicated. Of course she was after money. Girls like that always were.

"And then I was back on with the team," Bruce said, his water glass bouncing up and down so much that water splashed onto the threadbare carpet. "It was going well. We had a hell of a team! But then some assistant coach must have put steroids in my orange juice, man, because I tested positive at nationals. Can you *believe* that? And then I was off the team. Just like that." He tried snapping his fingers, but it made no sound. He tried again and managed it, but it was a feeble snap.

"They had a zero-tolerance policy?" I asked.

"Well, yeah. Kind of. I mean, there was some other stuff about conduct determinal to the team."

"Detrimental, you mean?"

"Yeah, yeah. Detrimental. That's right. It was all bullshit. It was me just horsing around with the guys, you know. Nothing serious. But a few of those guys are total sissies and they take everything personal."

He dropped his head and put his hand to his lips, holding it sideways as if sharing a secret. "Just between you and me, I think quite a few of them are faggots. I think they got into swimming just to see hot guys naked in the shower, know what I'm saying?"

The more he talked, the more I felt like a hole had opened up underneath me. The story I'd hoped to write, about the star high school athlete bound for the Olympics who'd been derailed by his father's death, was already falling apart. I should have known better. Bruce "Bigfoot" Garwood was exactly who he was in high school: an arrogant, entitled asshole who'd been blessed with great genes but no moral compass whatsoever. Nobody wanted to read about this guy. Even for a newspaper feature, it was way too depressing.

But I still clung to the father angle. Maybe there was something there. "You mentioned your Dad's will," I said. "Did he die while you were in college?"

"No, no, that was after I came home. See, he said maybe I should take a year off, you know. To regroup. So I did. I came home. And we had a plan. We did, man! He said he had an angle on getting me on the team at Oregon State. But then he had a heart attack. A big one, and he just didn't wake up one morning. A heart surgeon who died of a heart attack. Who ever heard of that? Shit."

He bowed his head, his mop of hair veiling his face. For just a second I thought this was it, I was going to get some honest emotion out of him, maybe a heartfelt soliloquy about how his dad meant everything to him, how if he'd had just one more chance, his dad might have helped him get him on the right track.

"The timing sucked," Bruce mumbled.

"What's that?"

He looked up at me. If there was moisture in his eyes, I couldn't see it, and the hard edge in his voice dispelled any thought I had that he was about to break down and get emotional with me. "The timing, it sucked big time. See, Dad married this bitch Yvette, and he left her almost everything. I mean, me and my brother and my sister all got some money, and a few things, like I got the Corvette, but it wasn't much. It didn't last long. Just a few years, you know?"

"Oh."

"You think maybe she'd offer to help me? No way. She said I had to grow up sometime. You believe that? Who needs her! I've got some things I'm working on. My cousin, he works for this tech company in Portland, and he said he can get me on in sales. And did I tell you about my blog? I review sports movies. I hadn't done one in a while because I got to get my Internet fixed, but as soon as I do, I'm back at it."

Bruce went on babbling about all the different angles he'd cooked up, all the different ways he was going to get his life back on track. I pretended to jot a few notes in my notebook, but I was barely listening to him anymore.

What really separated me and Bruce "Bigfoot" Garwood, anyway? Was my attitude that much better? I was sitting here in Felony Flats right next to him. I couldn't kid myself about where I was. Maybe my personality wasn't quite so toxic, but I knew I was well on my way. It wouldn't be long now.

At that moment, I heard an approaching train whistle, a few blocks over. I knew that sound well. Not all the trains were Amtraks, of course, but I always imagined they were, passenger trains ferrying people to better things, north to Washington, south to California, always something better, better people, better lives, richer, healthier, happier. Now here it was, making a special stop just to let me aboard.

But it was all a lie, wasn't it? It wasn't taking me to something better but instead to the past, back to that bedroom with those movie posters and mom crying in the other room and me just wishing, hoping, praying I could make something of myself so I didn't have to end up in a place like this again.

The gravitational pull, it was so strong. I finally realized there was no escape.

"You got anything around?" I asked Bruce.

He looked at me funny. When I spoke, my voice sounded detached. I was so tired. I didn't want to fight the inevitable anymore. Why not just let go? Embrace the real me. At least I'd have Bruce to keep me company. Maybe I could move in with him. Sleep on the couch. There was plenty of room.

"What?" he said.

"You know, to get in the creative mood?"

"Huh?"

"Come on," I said, "you know what I'm talking about. I bet you have something in that bag you brought in."

He didn't say anything.

"I'm telling you," I said, "there's a real movie here, I think. I just need something to help us get the ideas flowing. Did you know I wrote *Faraway and Forever?* I think there's something here just as good as that. I'm telling you."

For a long time, he just stared at me, then he finally bowed his head. I heard the train whistle again, closer now. I craved the release the drugs would bring.

Finally, Bruce got up and shuffled into the kitchen, his back to me. I figured he was going for his stash. The train was so close I heard it rattling over the tracks. He stood like that for a long time, this tall, rangy figure in the Hawaiian shirt and the Nike exercise pants. His head was bent slightly forward, and I could just imagine him about to dive into a pool.

Then he grabbed something out of the kitchen. I heard a metallic clatter, and then there he was looming over me.

Holding a steak knife.

The knife was a pitiful little thing with a wooden

handle and a rusty, serrated blade. It looked especially small in his oven-mitt hand, but it was still a knife, and quite capable of stabbing me in the heart—a heart that was now beating hard enough that I felt it all the way up in my throat.

"You can't have my drugs!" he cried.

"Jesus," I said, raising my arms, "it was just—just an idea—"

"If you try to take them, I'm going to cut you!"

I was in an extremely vulnerable position, glued to the couch, him looming over me as if looking for an excuse, any excuse, to jab me. "Okay, okay," I said. "Bruce, I'm not taking anything. Just don't—"

"Get up!"

"What?"

"Get up! Get up right now! Get off the couch!"

He feinted at me with the knife. I didn't want to stand but I didn't know what else to do. I got up, feeling shaky, my head spinning. He was going to kill me. I could see it in his eyes. I was dead.

"Listen," I said. "Bruce, buddy, listen to me. I'm not trying to steal your drugs. I just thought—"

"Shut up, shut up!" He squeezed his eyes closed, then shook his head so hard his big mane whipped left and right. "I knew you weren't stealing them! I knew that! But you can't have them. I'm not letting you. You're going places, man. You're going places, and I'm not—I'm not pulling you down with me."

I didn't know what to say to this. I was surprised, not just by his desire to protect me, but by his candor. For the first time since I'd been in his apartment, he'd been honest with me. *I'm not pulling you down with me.* Hadn't I said those exact words to Amy?

"I'm already gone," I said.

"No, you're not."

"I'm a junkie, just like you."

"Shut up!" He was crying now. "You're not like me. You've done something."

"Why do you think I'm here in Rexton? I washed out in Hollywood, man. I even lied about *Faraway and Forever.* That wasn't even my movie. They stole it from me, man. They stole it. I don't want to play their game anymore."

"Shut up! Just shut up! You just need somebody to lean on, that's all." His eyes flashed. "That girlfriend! The one who called you! What was her name?"

"No," I said.

"Amy! That was her name."

"She's not—"

"You should call Amy. You should tell her you need help."

"She's not my girlfriend anymore."

"She is, she is! She wouldn't call if she wasn't! Now get up. You're leaving. You're leaving, and the first thing you're going to do is call her."

"Bruce—"

He jabbed his knife toward me, the tails of his Hawaiian shirt fluttering behind him. I stepped back.

He grabbed my bag and thrust it into my arms, pushing me backward, all the way to his door.

"I don't got anybody, Chris," he said. "Don't you see? Nobody at all. But you got somebody. Call her and tell her you want to come home."

"Rexton is my home."

"No, it isn't. Not anymore. Now go. Go, or I'm going to kill you, dammit!"

He jabbed the knife closer. My back pushed against the door. His eyes, so dark and wide, flashed through the smog of his hair. As he crowded near me, he was so tall he blocked the light behind him, casting me in shadow, and the knife point glinted. It was inches from my neck.

Somehow I got the knob turned. I fell backwards, grabbing onto the Buddha statue as I went, and slammed against the wooden railing. He took one step out, glaring at me, swiping at the air with his knife.

"Call her!" he screamed after me.

Then he slammed the door.

I lay like that for a long time, hugging the Buddha statue, the cold boards pressing against my back. I heard what sounded like sobbing, and I thought about trying the door, talking to him, finding our way back to just two guys shooting the breeze, but the thought of the knife stopped me.

Then I heard the train whistle again, far off now, almost gone.

At some point I stumbled down the stairs. It had

gotten colder. As the heat dissipated from my body, the chill air pressed in from all sides. Not far away, inside a house somewhere, I heard children's laughter. A raccoon darted under the Winnebago.

By the time I made it to the Mustang, I was breathing again, and my heart no longer felt like it was going to burst from my chest. When the dome light faded, I sat in the dark car, surrounded by all those houses, the houses of my youth. The past and the future. It was all here.

I didn't know what to do, but I knew that Bruce Garwood had been right about one thing, at least. Screenwriting was my creative vice. It may have put me through the wringer, but I didn't want to give it up. I also knew I couldn't do it alone.

I took out my cell phone. Dialed. Waited a beat. What if she didn't pick up? What if she'd finally given up on me?

When she answered, I knew she hadn't. Not yet. I could hear it in her voice. It was just the word hello, but the tone said it all. I didn't know what to say, so I said the most obvious thing and hoped we'd figure out the rest.

"I need your help," I said.

<hr>

I RETURNED THE FOLLOWING CHRISTMAS, more than a year later, to visit my mother. The pandemic was raging by this point. Trump was out of office. Everybody was wearing masks. It was a different world. This time I brought Amy, and she was now sporting a diamond engagement ring.

I'd been completely sober, gainfully employed, and I was starting to think my own comeback was the real deal. In addition to my work with the sitcom, I'd started noodling around with a few spec scripts. We went out for coffee with Rick and his wife, who turned out to be a fan of *Joey Knows!* I could even claim I wrote some of her favorite lines.

But even if I hadn't, even if nothing I'd written ended up on the screen, that would have been fine, too. Just like Officer Brady, I was doing my best. I was finally figuring out how to be okay with that being enough.

Afterwards, I took Amy on a tour of my old neighborhood, puttering through the dark streets of Felony Flats in Mom's Mustang with the sagging telephone wires and the cars on cinderblocks. I pointed out my childhood home. I pointed out where I used to sit near the train tracks and watch the Amtraks go by. I pointed out where I called Amy last November, the moment when everything changed.

I almost didn't stop at Bruce's apartment, not sure how he'd react to seeing me again, but I couldn't help myself. I wanted to thank him.

There was no Buddha statue at the top of the stairs, and the man who answered the door was not Bruce Garwood. He was an old guy with white hair and a big belly that pressed against his camo shirt—a sort of beardless Santa Claus if Santa Claus had fought in Vietnam and now stood on two metal legs. He wore a blue surgical mask, and I wished I'd remembered to put on my own mask before I'd clambered up the steps, but it was too late now.

"Bruce?" he said, his voice muffled by the thin cloth. He was holding onto the frame for support. I smelled pizza and heard a football game. "I'm sorry, man. He OD'd a couple months back. Neighbor found him. I'm sorry to break the news to you."

It hit me harder than I thought it would, probably because I never thought it would happen to him. He was Bruce "Bigfoot" Garwood, after all, star swimmer, bound for great things, and now his story had ended. I knew I'd never write it. This little tale? It's just for Amy, a way to thank her for allowing me back into her life, and because she asked why I eventually called. It's up to her if she wants to share it with others.

My opinion? The world doesn't need anymore stories about the guys that didn't make it. There are plenty of those. I used to be one of them.

I might *still* be one of them, if it weren't for Bruce.

ABOUT THE AUTHOR

SCOTT WILLIAM CARTER's first novel was hailed by *Publishers Weekly* as a "touching and impressive debut" and won an Oregon Book Award. Since then, he has published dozens of books, including the popular Garrison Gage mystery series set on the Oregon coast. His book for younger readers, *Wooden Bones*, chronicles the untold story of Pinocchio and was singled out for praise by the Junior Library Guild. In past lives, he has been an academic technologist, a writing instructor, bookstore owner, the manager of a computer training company, and a ski instructor, though the most important job—and best —he's ever had is being the father of his two children. He lives with his family in Oregon.

Visit him online at
www.ScottWilliamCarter.com

Dead-Eyed Drifter

Other Books for Adults

The Dinosaur Diaries

A Web of Black Widows

The Man Who Made No Mistakes

Ask Hagan

Looking for Little Red

Young Adult Novels

The Last Great Getaway of the Water Balloon Boys

President Jock, Vice President Geek

The Care and Feeding of Rubber Chickens

Books for All Ages

Drawing a Dark Way

A Tale of Two Giants

Wooden Bones

The Castle on the Hill at the Edge of the World

The Dragon Lottery

www.ingramcontent.com/pod-product-compliance
Lightning Source LLC
Chambersburg PA
CBHW030141010826
48973CB00002B/671